CATTLE

WINNIFRED EATON
AKA ONOTO WATANNA

Invisible Publishing
Halifax & Toronto

Library and Archives Canada Cataloguing in Publication

Title: Cattle / by Winnifred Eaton, A.K.A. Onoto Watanna.

Names: Eaton, Winnifred, 1875-1954, author.

Description: Series statement: Throwback books ; 6

Originally published: Toronto: Musson, 1923.

Identifiers: Canadiana (print) 20230167551 | Canadiana (ebook) 20230167675 | ISBN 9781778430244 (softcover) | ISBN 9781778430251 (HTML)

Classification: LCC PS8459.A86 C3 2023 | DDC C813/.52—dc23

Throwback series editor: Bart Vautour
Cover artwork, cover design, and interior design: Megan Fildes
Typeset in Laurentian, with thanks to type designer Rod McDonald

Invisible Publishing is committed to protecting our natural environment. As part of our efforts, both the cover and interior of this book are printed on acid-free 100% post-consumer recycled fibres.

Printed and bound in Canada

Invisible Publishing | Halifax & Toronto
www.invisiblepublishing.com

Published with the generous assistance of the Canada Council for the Arts, the Ontario Arts Council, and the Government of Canada.

AN INTRODUCTION TO *CATTLE*

by Lily Cho

Cattle is the novel that Winnifred Eaton's publishers did not want to publish. It is a major departure from her earlier, commercially successful novels and stories. While Eaton recounts her publishers lamenting the brutality of the story, they also grappled with the problem of selling a novel that is devoid of the Japanese or Chinese American characters and themes through which Eaton and her sister, Edith Maude Eaton (who wrote under the name Sui Sin Far) had become famous. Eaton's previous novels drew from her Chinese and British ancestry. While her sister Edith's writing focused on Chinese and Chinese American characters, Winnifred's writing featured Japanese and Japanese American heroines and themes. Although she was born in Canada and lived much of her life in Canada, *Cattle*, first published in 1923, is one of only two novels in Eaton's oeuvre that is set in Canada. The other, *His Royal Nibs* (1925), is also about life in the Canadian West. Of the two though, *Cattle* is distinct for the courage of its darkness.

In *Cattle*, Eaton whisks her readers away to a place as strange and new as any she has taken them before: a cattle ranch in Alberta run by a violent and brutish rancher named Bull Langdon. As his name suggests, Langdon's character is larger-than-life. He dominates the rooms he steps into and the people in them. However, in many ways, the real star of the novel is Nettie, a teenaged orphan who works as a domestic helper on the ranch. Nettie's resourcefulness and deep goodness shine against the starkness of life on a cattle ranch in early twentieth century Alberta. The novel is not propelled by Bull Langdon's ruthlessness, but rather by following how Nettie carves hope out of hopelessness.

Cattle has been repeatedly referred to as a page-turner. The novel began as a synopsis for a film script, based on a true story that Eaton heard after she had moved to Alberta to live on a ranch in the foothills of the Rocky Mountains. It is filmic in its pacing, dialogue, and vivid scene-setting. Eaton loved riding her horse alone across the foothills and the depth of her feeling for the prairies is threaded throughout the novel.

Terrible things do happen in this novel. There is illness and death, violence and, particularly, sexual violence. While we cannot look away from the horrors that are a part of the novel, it does ask important questions about what justice looks like in a place and time when so many wrongs cannot be made right through formal means. Eaton demands much more of her characters, and of her readers, than mere acquiescence to situations of profound inequity and injustice. There is a kind of justice that unfolds in the novel where some wrongs are not exactly made right — indeed, Eaton shows her readers every wrong cannot be righted — but wrongdoers are still brought into the thrall of suffering.

While Eaton was, in many ways, ahead of her time in terms of her depiction of the challenges and struggles that her women characters faced, she was very much of her time in terms of her representation of Indigenous peoples and racialized others. Eaton is often understood by academics as a writer who humanized racial others, particularly Asian Americans, in that she was one of the first mixed race Canadian authors to write about racialized characters. Through Eaton, Anglophone readers got stories of romance and adventure where the central characters were Japanese and Japanese American. Still, to contemporary readers, these depictions are reminders that good intentions can carry with them their own problems and biases. Nevertheless, Eaton recognizes in *Cattle* that Western Canada is not a purely white space and writes into the novel the diversity of people and culture that she encountered in her own life.

Canada is a settler colonial nation and *Cattle* gives to readers some of the texture of the viciousness that is part and parcel of what it means to colonize a place when colonizers take land that is not theirs to take, operate businesses, start families, and build communities in a place that does not belong to them. Settlement can sound benign. *Cattle* is a riveting reminder that the act of settlement is a violent process. It is a form of theft and it leaves Canadians living under the long shadow of that wrong. The novel does not give its readers a long view of these wrongs. It takes us into the heart of them and bring us up close to the violence and pain that haunts Canada still.

Finally, reading *Cattle* in the wake of the mass death event that is the COVID-19 pandemic, there is a new poignancy to Eaton's narration of the arrival of the Spanish Flu, or more precisely, the Great Influenza Pandemic of 1918, in the latter part of the novel. Eaton's story of the pandemic offers a potently fresh view of the one that would be unleashed on the world a century later. Readers can follow a little-told story of the pandemic then and the pandemic now: that of its effects on rural and isolated communities. Stories of pandemics and plagues have tilted toward tracking sites of population density and the spread of the disease in places where people are most closely clustered such as cities and, in our contemporary era, cruise ships and airports. How a plague travels when people live far away from each other, far from the concentrations of medical expertise and supplies in urban areas, is a story that has not been told enough.

Although the novel is not primarily about a plague, the influenza pandemic catalyzes every thread of the plot. Eaton's plague is neither a metaphor nor a historical event in the backdrop of the novel. It is both anchor and destroyer. Here, the plague ushers in justice for the novel's central characters and sets to some right that which had been wrong. Writing in March 2020, during that frantic early period of the Covid-19 pandemic, Jill Lepore declared, "Every plague novel is a parable." Riffing on Camus, Lepore goes on to argue that the "plague novel is the place where all human beings abandon all other human beings." And yet, Eaton's novel insists upon the opposite of abandonment. The novel's heroes run into known danger. *Cattle* tells its readers that abandonment is not the answer. Against the idea of Canadian literature as thematically bound to survival, Eaton tells us that survival is not enough.

The publication history of this novel gives readers a window into the complex ways that Eaton's identity circulated in North America and Britain. The novel was first published in Great Britain in 1923 by Hutchinson & Co, under the pen name Onoto Watanna, then published in Canada the same year by Musson, again under the name Onoto Watanna. The book was then published in the USA by W.J. Watt in 1924 under the name Winnifred Eaton (Onota Watonna) [sic]. The pseudonym in the parenthesis of the US edition may first appear to be a typo but the book certainly circulated with that odd spelling on top of the established oddity of her more established pseudonym, Onoto Watanna. Long before *Cattle* was published, Eaton had wanted to begin to publish under her own name and to move away from the Japanese-inflected authorial identity she had developed. The many different versions of her name attached to this novel across three different national contexts offers some sense of the difficulty of that transition. There are no clean breaks between her Japanese persona and the Anglocentrism of her given name. Her Chinese heritage remains invisible in all of her names. Throughout her life, Eaton's identities continue to converge and complicate her identity as a writer.

Winnifred Eaton is one of the most important North American writers of the early twentieth century. She was incredibly prolific. She did not hide her mixed-race identity, despite the racism of her time. She brought into the world some of the earliest stories of Asian and Asian American women in English-language literature. Given Eaton's incredible legacy, *Cattle* is uniquely important. It is the first time that she writes a novel about Canada. *Cattle* is also one of the earliest novels of Western Canada in Canadian literature. It is also rare in that it takes readers to one of the most important cultural and economic sites in this part of the world: the cattle ranch. *Cattle* takes far more risks than *His Royal Nibs*. *Cattle* is a darker story, daring to bring readers to a less comfortable and, I would argue, much more interesting place. For a writer who spent her entire career writing with a canny understanding of how to give readers stories that they wanted, and thus what stories would sell, Eaton gambles here on a story with a hard edge. After decades of what she termed "fairy-like stories of Japan," it is with *Cattle* that Eaton finally begins to write "tales of the things and people I have known" (Birchall). She decided, with *Cattle*, that she would write with the "strong, hot pen of a man" (Birchall). Readers of *Cattle* can celebrate the emergence of Winnifred Eaton as a writer who fought to finally tell a story of a life that she knew and with a voice that carries the clarity and strength of the fullness of that knowing.

SOURCES

Birchall, Diana, "Winnifred Eaton." *The Dictionary of Literary Biography.* Gale Cengage Learning, 2009.

Lepore, Jill, "What Our Contagion Fables are Really About." *The New Yorker.* March 23, 2020.

CHAPTER I

FOUR ALBERTA RANCHES are concerned in this tale. Of these three were quarter sections of land in Yankee Valley, and the fourth, the vast Bar Q, whose area of over two hundred thousand acres of rich grain, hay, and grazing lands, began on the prairie and extended into the foothills of the Rocky Mountains. Here, spreading over the best of the grazing lands and the Chinook-swept slopes, where all winter long the cattle grazed as in summer time, its jealous fingers, like those of a miser that begrudges a pinch of his gold, reached across into the Indian Reserve.

For many years the Bar Q cattle had the right of way over the Indian lands, the agents that came and went, finding it more profitable to work in the interests of the cowman, than those of mere Indians. Like all the rest of the country thereabouts, including the Indians themselves, they presently came under the power, and were swept into the colossal "game" of the man who was known throughout the country as "The Bull," owner of the Bar Q.

Few recalled when first the Bull, or, to give him his proper name, Bill Langdon, came into the foothills. His brand blazed out bold and huge before the trails were staked and the railroads were pushing their noses into the new land. Even at that early period his covetous eye had marked the Indian cattle, "rolling fat" as the term is in the cattle world, and smugly grazing over the rich pasture lands, with the "I.D." (Indian Department) brand upon their right ribs, a warning to "rustlers" from east and west and south and north, that these were the property of the Canadian Government.

Little cared Bull Langdon for the Canadian Government, and he spat contemptuously at the word. Bull had come hastily out of Montana, and, although he had flouted and set at defiance the laws of his native land, away from it, he chose to regard with supreme contempt all other portions of the earth that were not included in the great Union across the line.

His first Cattle were "Rustled" from the unbranded Indian calves, and driven to convenient forest corrals by renegade members of the tribe, who traded them to the Cow-Man for the desired drink.

Though the rustling of Indian cattle proved remunerative and easy, he by no means overlooked or despised the cattle of the early pioneers, nor the fancy fat stuff imported into the country by the English "remittance men."

Slowly the Bar Q herd grew in size and quality. With the growth of his herd, Bull Langdon acquired life-leases upon thousands of acres of government land—forest and Indian Reserve. Closing in upon discouraged and impoverished homesteaders and pioneers, he bought what he could not steal.

Somewhere, somehow, the Bull had come upon a phrase of ancient days that appealed vastly to his greedy and vain imagination.

"The cattle on a thousand hills are mine!" he gloated, and roared aloud another favourite boast:

"There ain't no cattle on two or four legs that Bull Langdon fears."

He was a man of gigantic stature, with a coarse, brutalized face that had an element of primitive savagery about its expression.

The name "Bull" had been applied to him because of his bellowing voice, his great strength and his driving methods with his men and his cattle. Tyrannical, unprincipled and cruel, Bull was hated and feared. He had fought his way to the top by the sheer force of his raging, dominating personality. On top he reigned mercilessly, arrogantly and unscrupulously.

To him, cattle and men were akin. Most men, he asserted, were "scrub" stock, and went up tamely and submissively before the branding iron. A minority were spirited and thoroughbred. For these the squeezegate had been invented, and those who were not therein "broke," emerged crippled or were killed. Finally, there were the mavericks, wild stuff, that, escaping the lariat of the cowpuncher, roamed the range unbranded. For these outlaws the Bull had a measure of respect. There was a double bounty for every head of such stuff rolled into the Bar Q. Quite often the Bull himself joined in the dangerous and exciting chase.

If the Bull considered men of the same breed as cattle, he had less respect for the female of the human species. With few exceptions he snarled, spitting with contempt, women were "scrub" stock, easy "stuff," that could be whistled or driven to home pastures. A man had but to reach out and help himself to what he desired.

In somewhat this mood, he had overruled the alarmed objections of the timid, gentle girl from Ontario, who had taught in the rural school planted in the heart of the then stern and rigid country. It is true he had thrown no lariat over the neck of the school teacher, for he had no wish to kill what he coveted; but the cowman knew of diabolical traps more ingenious than the squeezegate into which a girl's unwary feet might be ensnared.

She was an innocent, harmless creature, weak and devoted, the kind that is born to mother things. The years had given Mrs. Langdon only dreams to mother—dreams of babies that came with every year, only to be snuffed out, when on some barren homestead she fought out her agony and longing alone and unhelped.

Time had never accustomed the wife of the cattleman to these fearful losses. Always she clung to the hope that the Bull would send her, in time, to the city—Calgary. Those were the years, however, when the Bull had no time nor thought for a mere wife. He was of the breed that sits up all night long with a sick cow, or rides the range in search of a lost one, but is indifferent and callous to the suffering of his own mate. Those were the years when he was building up his herd. He was buying and stealing land and cattle. He was drunk with a dream of conquest and power, intent upon climbing to the top. His ambition was to be the cattle king of Alberta—the "King Pin" of the north-west country.

The years of power and affluence came too late to help the wife of the cattleman. Mrs. Langdon reached a period when she could no longer bear a child. Yet the maternal instinct which dominated her nature reached out to mother the children of neighbouring ranchers, the rosy-cheeked papooses on the little squaws' backs, the rough lads who worked upon the ranch, and to find room in her heart even for the half-witted illegitimate son of the Bull.

Jake was a half-breed, whose infirmity was due to a blow from his father, when, as a boy, upon the death of his mother on the Indian Reserve, Jake had come to the Bar Q and ingenuously claimed the Bull as his father. As far as lay in her power, Mrs. Langdon sought to compensate to the unfortunate half-breed for the man's cruelty, and it was her gentle influence—she was newly married to the Bull at that time—that prevailed upon him to permit Jake to continue upon the ranch. Here he worked about the house, doing the chores and the wood-chopping and the carrying of water. He was slavishly devoted to his stepmother, and he kept out of the way of the heavy hand and foot of the Bull, for whom he entertained a wholesome dread.

CHAPTER II

HOWEVER BULL LANGDON MUST DOMINATE THIS STORY, for the present we return to the three humble quarter sections aforementioned.

The first of these, one hesitates to name ranch or farm. It was known as the "D.D.D.," the "D's" being short for "Dan Day Dump," a name applied to the place by a neighbouring farmer, which had ever afterwards stuck.

It was on the extreme rocky edge of Yankee Valley, an otherwise prosperous part of the prairie country, so named because most of its settlers hailed from the U.S.A.

Dan Day himself had come from the States, but he had acquired a wife in Canada. They "fetched up" finally at this sorry "stopping-off place," as they called it then, where first they squatted, and then, through the medium of neighbours interested in keeping the shiftless new-comers from encroaching upon the more fertile lands hard by, they staked their homestead. Here Dan Day erected the rackety shack and lean-to, in which his growing family and stock found a sort of shelter. In the main, the Day children grew like Indians.

Time had taught the homesteader at least one lesson, namely, that a living could not be squeezed from his barren acres. Day, as his neighbours were wont to declare, shaking a condemning head, was not cut out to be a farmer. Nevertheless, they gave him grudging employment, and his incompetent services were endured largely because the community waged an uncompromising warfare against the stern approach of school authorities, who had begun to question whether the size of the Day family did not warrant the imposition upon the municipality of a new rural school.

Howbeit, time and growth are things the farmer must, most of all men, reckon with, and even as the crops leaped tall and strong from the new black virgin soil, even as the cattle and stock grew in flesh and number, and spread out and multiplied over the pasture lands of Alberta, so shot upward the Day progeny, and seemed, hungrily, to demand and question their place in the world.

There were ten of them. A baby—and there was always a baby in that family—of a few months, a toddler of two, another of three, another of five, twins of seven, a boy of nine, twins of twelve, and Nettie, aged fourteen at the time her mother died, leaving in the girl's hands the appalling problem of fending and caring for the wild brood of hungry young ones.

Nettie was of that blonde type seen more often in the northern lands. She was a big girl, with milk-white skin and dead gold hair. A slow-moving, slow-thinking girl, simple and ignorant of the world outside that which bounded the narrow confines of their homestead land. School, as mentioned above, had played no part in the life of Nettie Day. She knew vaguely of books and papers; she had seen, but could not read them. She thought that in this world of ours there were two kinds of folk, those who were rich and those who were poor. The rich lived away off somewhere on big ranches, where the cattle were fat and the grain grew high, though some lived also in the cities. Nettie had heard of cities. Her father had come from a small town in Oregon. As for the poor folk, simply, resignedly, Nettie accepted the fact that they, the Days, were of the poor. Life for them was an eternal struggle against hunger and cold.

Occasionally certain neighbouring farmers riding the range or bringing home stray cattle, dropped into the Day homestead and shared the meagre meal shyly set out by Nettie. In the latter years, as the girl burst into a sort of potential bloom, the neighbours lingered a bit to stare curiously at this maturing product of the "D.D.D." Also, Nettie possessed one true and unfailing friend, he who had brought her and her nine little brothers and sisters into the world; who came periodically to scold, tease and teach, to clean and work in an effort to bring some semblance of order into the chaotic confusion that reigned in that shack, which housed twelve living souls.

Dr. McDermott, though twenty years in Canada, was as stubbornly Scotch as on the day he landed. His practice extended from the prairie to the mountains. He had brought into the world a majority of the children who had arrived in that part of the country since he had planted his own rough homestead in their midst. There were other equally homeless and dependent families for the "Doc" to scold and instruct, and not often did he find time to talk to Nettie. She would plan out questions she intended to put to him upon the occasion of his monthly visit, but, slow and shy, by the time the doctor would be through with his condemning inspection of the family mode of life, the questions would escape her.

"Growing! Growing! Growing!" would growl the Scotch doctor, glaring about the circle of healthy, grimy faces— "like weeds! like weeds!" Latterly, however, like the neighbours, his glance rested longer upon Nettie, and once his brows puckered, he changed the "weed" to "flower." He likened Nettie Day's growth to that of a flower—a wild flower. She liked the thought that her doctor friend had picked her out, as it were, from the weeds, and her bosom swelled with pride when he appeared unexpectedly at the shack and took her with him across the country to help care for the sick woman in the shack on the quarter section, which had been Dr. McDermott's own original homestead.

That swift running drive over the road allowances in the doctor's democrat, stood out always in the memory of Nettie, as one of the few sweet days of her life.

It was early March, but a "Chinook" (warm wind, which has its origin in the Japanese current) had melted all of the flying snow of a March blizzard. Miracle-like had been the effects of that warm wind. It had sunk deep into the earth and thawed the last bit of frost from the ground. Streams were running along the roads, the sloughs were filling to the brim, the cattle no longer nibbled in the neighbourhood of the fenced-in hay and straw stacks, but bit down into the upshooting grass, green already in this remarkable land. Eight-horse teams were pulling plough, disc and harrow out into the fields, preparatory for an early seeding. Overhead, a great, warm sun sent its benevolent rays abroad, tinting sky and earth with a warm glow. The land, indeed, was bathed in sunlight. Small wonder that someone had fondly named it: "Sunny Alberta, the Land of Promise."

If Nettie was slow of speech and shy, Dr. McDermott was Scotch and brief. There was that, moreover, upon his mind at this time, that dismayed and concerned him deeply. It is not strange, therefore, that as he whipped his horses to their top speed—they were on an errand that in his professional judgment meant a matter of life or death—he forgot the girl at his side, looking about her in a sort of rapt trance.

All the world seemed good and bonny to Nettie at this time. Life was thrilling. The bumping, rickety old democrat was a coach of luxury, the rough trails and road allowances, full of holes and mud sloughs, a smooth highway over which she was being borne into a scene that spelled romance.

She had more than ever an opportunity to gaze out to where far across the horizon the mighty peaks of the Rocky Mountains traced their fingers of snow. Always the hills stirred something that was vaguely yearning, that thrilled, even while it pained. Prairie born, and prairie raised, she aspired to the hills. She knew not why, except that the hills lifted one up—up—up—into the clouds themselves. She had a childlike faith that "something good" would come to her out

14

of the hills. That "something good" she had recognized, with rapture, to be the young rider from the great Bar Q who had spent a never-to-be-forgotten hour at the "D.D.D." in the fall.

For several days long files of the Bar Q cattle had been trailing down from the hill country. They were being driven from the summer range in the foothills to the grain ranches on the prairie. Here, beneath the shelter of the long cattle sheds, or loose in the sunlit pastures where were the great straw and hay stacks, the mothers of the famous herd were especially housed and nurtured during the winter months, in preparation for the spring crop of calves.

This animal fall movement was an exciting event in the lives of the young Days. The children kept a count of every head of cattle that passed along the road, and there was great excitement and glee the following spring, when the herd returned to the foothills, with the pretty white-faced calves "at heel."

Nettie was no less thrilled than her small brothers and sisters by the advent of the Bar Q cattle, and up to the time of her mother's death she had scrambled with them under and over barbed wire fences, and scampered across pasture land to reach the road in time to see the cattle pour by. After her mother's death, things had changed. The babies kept her closely to the house, and the best she could do was to get as far as the edge of the corrals, a baby tucked under either arm, and toddlers clinging to her skirts. Here, standing upon a rail, she would call across to the flying youngsters her admonitions to be "careful."

That fall, however, hankering to see again the great herd from the hills, as it passed to the lower lands, Nettie scrubbed the faces of her grimy brood, arrayed them in clean jumpers made from bleached flour sacks, piled them aboard the old hay wagon, to which "Tick," a brother of thirteen, had already harnessed the team of geldings, and taking up the reins in her competent hands, she started for the trail.

Nettie was a big girl, with the softly maturing figure of a young Juno. She looked more than her fifteen years. Her hair was as gold as the Alberta sunlight, and the sun, aided and abetted by the anticipation and excitement, had whipped a splash of red into each rounded cheek. She had wide blue eyes, and they smiled back at the palpably moved riders, as she drove her wagon-load of tow-headed children out into the road. The eyes of the riders brightened and popped; wide hats and flowing ties were adjusted, as they rode on in the sunlight, whistling and singing and whirling a loose lariat in the hand. More than one of that outfit mentally made a note of the desirability of seeking strayed cattle in the near neighbourhood of the "D.D.D.", and when the last of the herd disappeared down the grade, a single horseman rode out of the bush and paused alongside the Day wagon.

His face was broad, sunburned, freckled, tough and ruddy. He had a wide, friendly smile, and a straight look out of the clear type of eyes one sees often in Western Canada, the eyes of one used to seeing over great distances, with a look of the outdoors and the freshness of youth and honesty about them. The way he released his wide hat from his head and held it over the pummel of his saddle, had something of unconscious grace and native courtliness about it, and the thick crop of brown hair, stirring in the slight wind, so that it blew back and raised on his head, gave him a singularly boyish look.

Had any in the Day wagon seen a roan heifer? "She" had given him a "sight of trouble." Got into the bush a half a mile down the grade, and "banged if she didn't get plumb out o' sight somewhere in the willows."

None in the Day wagon had seen the roan heifer, and the inquirer, screwing up his face, and scratching the side of his neck, ruminated in puzzled wonder as to the whereabouts of the missing animal, his eyes meanwhile resting full upon the lifted, glowing face of the girl in the driver's seat.

While conjecture and suggestion ran wildly out of the group of boys and girls, the rider sat up suddenly alert, and pointing towards some invisible speck, which he declared was "back of the shack there," he touched spurs to the flank of his bronco and was off toward the house after the elusive lost one. But when the wagon pulled up into the barnyard, and the children and Nettie scrambled down, and came across the yard to the house, they found the cowpuncher sitting disconsolately on the step, fanning himself with his great hat. Shaking his head to the shouted queries of the Day boys as to whether he had found "her," he replied:

"Nope. Guess she's flewed the coop. Gosh! but I'm hungry. Guess I'd better hop along and catch up with the bunch before they bolt all o' the grub."

That remark, needless to say, brought a clamouring invitation from the young Days for dinner, and after the usual remonstrance for the trouble he'd be making, and a questioning, rather wistful look toward Nettie, who shyly seconded the children's invitation, he "guessed"—"well, mebbe I will, though don't go to any trouble for me."

Trouble! That acceptance sent Nettie flying about the mean room, her cheeks aflame, her eyes shining, and her heart singing like a bird's within her, while the children crowded about their guest, who, in his buckskin shirt, fur chaps, gauntlets and cowboy hat, appeared a hero to the young prairie eyes.

It may, however, be recorded that Nettie was by no means the only one through whose veins an exhilarating elixir seemed to be bounding like champagne. Young Cyril Stanley, at that moment, was violently aware of a thumping organ in his left side.

Love knows not time. It wells up in the human heart like the waves of the ocean that may not be beaten down. Nettie Day, hurrying about that kitchen, preparing a meal for the hungry stranger, and that stranger himself, a "kid" on either knee, and the others pressed as closely to him as space would allow, displaying his big jack-knife, quirt, beaded hat-band and ticking watch, to the impressed youngsters, looked across the space of that poor and meagre room at each other, and felt, though they could not have expressed it in words, that somehow life had become a poem, a glad, dancing song that would run along forever.

CHAPTER III

THAT WINTER WAS LONG AND HARSH, with scarcely a Chinook to temper the intense cold. To Nettie, vainly trying to check the tide of work, noise and disorder, which the shutting in of a dozen husky youngsters must inevitably entail, and to Cyril Stanley, conscientiously at work in the pure-bred camp of the Bar Q, the Alberta winter had never seemed so long and grim. Cyril, however, found an outlet for the new feelings that he did not find hard to analyse. An Ontario born boy, of pure Scotch ancestry, he was both sentimental and practical. Though he had met her but once, he was assured that Nettie was the one girl in the world for him, and with a canny eye to the near future, he began immediately the preparations for the realization of his dreams. It did not take Cyril long to make application for the quarter section homestead land, which lay midway between the Day place and Dr. McDermott's original homestead. The savings of several years were prudently expended upon barbed wire and fence posts.

Though the best roper and rider of the Bar Q, and in line for the post of foreman of that tempestuous ranch, Cyril's faith was in the grain land, and he purposed to level up his homestead as soon as he could afford to do so. By sacrificing a certain amount of his pay, he would leave the Bar Q in the slack seasons and put in so much work per year upon his place. Already he possessed a few head of cattle and horse, and he planned to trade some of these for implements. He would begin the building of the house in the summer, after the fencing was done. Of the house, the boy thought long and lingeringly that winter. He had the heart and home hunger of the man in the ranching country who has come little into contact with women, but craves and longs for their companionship. Cyril's longing was enhanced by the fact that for the first time in his life he was in love. He pictured Nettie in his house, saw her moving about preparing their meal, thrilled at the thought of the meeting of their eyes and the touch of her hand in his. She would light up the whole place.

Dreams these—dreams that kept the formerly easy-tongued Cyril dumb and still, and aroused the good-natured query of the boys in the bunk-houses. Little cared Cyril for their jokes. Well he knew that the spring would come on apace, and then——!

Spring, in fact, came early that year, ushered in miraculously on the wings of a magnificent Chinook, which blew without ceasing for four days and nights, its warm breath hovering over a land so lately bitterly cold.

Nettie, driving along the road in the doctor's democrat, turned about in the seat to stare, with mild wonder, at the three rolls of barbed wire and the heaped up willow fence posts that were piled on the unbroken quarter by which they were now passing

"My!" said Nettie, "Looks like someone's took up this quarter. D'you know who they are, Doc?"

"Let's see. Seems to me I did hear that a Bar Q hand had staked there."

At the word "Bar Q," such a rush of colour flooded the girl's face, that, had the doctor been less intent upon driving the lagging team at a speed they were totally unused to, he might have surprised the girl's secret. But Dr. McDermott's eyes were fastened steadily ahead to where, across the bald-headed prairie, his own first home in Alberta poked its head up against the skyline. He was in a hurry to reach that long deserted shack.

From up the grade, the figure of a horseman beeame silhouetted against the sun. Nettie's heart began to beat so frantically that she was obliged to grip the sleeve of the doctor's coat.

"That's right," he growled, "hold on tight. These roads are a mortal disgrace—a disgrace to the community."

"Whip up," he hailed the rider, stopping long enough to give Cyril an opportunity to join them.

"How do, Doc! Business good?"

The rider had awkwardly lifted his hat, but his eyes jumped as he perceived who it was that was riding with the doctor, while over the girl's cheeks there came a flush like the dawn.

"C'n I do anything for you, Doc? Everything all right?"

"Nothing's right. Look at this road. It's an eternal disgrace—a disgrace to the community."

Dr. McDermott "cussed" heartily and without measure.

"Should've made the grade in quarter the time."

"Where you bound for? Shall I ride along with you?"

"You may. Might need you. Sick wom———" He started to say "woman," and then changed and blurted out "'lady,' over there."

"You don't say. Not at your old dump? Well, what's she doing there? Shall I go ahead, Doc?"

"She owns the place. Don't know what may have happened or when she arrived. Drove by this morning. Saw the door down and the nails off the window. Went in, and—well, it's a sick woman—a very sick woman. Get up, you, Mack!"

He rumbled angry reproaches to the lagging horses.

Cyril rode close to the left hand side of the democrat, his fur chaps at times brushing the girl. They looked at each other, flushed, turned away and looked back. For some time they rode along in this electrical silence, tongue-tied but content. Conversation at last bubbled forth, but they spoke not of that which filled to the top both of their young hearts, but of the common topics of the ranching country.

"Well, how's things at the D.D.D.?"

"Not too bad. How's things at Bar Q?"

"Jake-a-loo. Stock in plumb good shape. Two hundred and eighty calves dropped already. Expectin' all of two thousand this spring."

"Two thousand calves! Oh my! That's an awful sight of cattle." She sighed. "We just got six head."

"That's not too bad. Bull Langdon started with less than that. I got twenty head of my own. Hope to ketch up with the Bull by'n by."

They laughed heartily at that. Not so much because they saw wit and brilliance in the remark, but because their hearts were young, the spring had come, the sun was above and it was good to hear each other's voices and to look into each other's eyes.

"What's your brand?"

"Mine? You don't say you never seen it yet?"

Again they went off into a happy gale.

"It's a circle on the left rib. Gotter look out. Bar Q's pretty much the same. All the Bull's got to do to my circle is to make a click to turn it into a 'Q' and brand a bar above that. Pretty easy, huh?"

"Oh-h, but he wouldn't do a thing like that!"

She was startled, palpably alarmed in his behalf, and that alarm was sweet and dear to him.

"Wouldn't he, though! Sa-ay, where've you been living all your days that you never heard how the Bull got his herd?"

"Oh, my, I did hear once, but I didn't suppose that now he's so rich and owns half the cattle in the country, that he'd do such things to-day."

"Oh, wouldn't he, though! Just give'm half a chance. He's got the habit, you see, and habits is like our skin, they stick to us."

Again they laughed merrily at this witticism.

"Orders are," went on Cyril, expanding under the flattering attention paid him, and the shy admiration that shone in Nettie's wide blue eyes, to lick in any and all stuff runnin' loose around the country—unbranded stuff, and stuff where the brand ain't clear. He give me the tip himself. Said there'd be a five to the rider for every head rolled in.

Of course I'm not losing sleep about my stuff. I know just where they are on the range, you betcha, and I'm not leavin' them out o' sight too long. Thinkin' of tradin' them in, anyway, for—for —lumber and implements.

"Lumber?" she repeated innocently.

"Yep. Goin' to build."

His gaze sank deeply into Nettie's, and her heart rose up, and then stood still in her breast.

"Wh-what are you building?" she asked in a breathless whisper, so that he had to bend down from his horse to catch the question; and the answer came with a rich boy laugh:

"A *home*, girl!"

After that ecstatic sentence, and as if to relieve some of his pent-up joyful feelings, Cyril rode forward at a quick canter, raced on ahead and raced back again, to bring up beside the slow-travelling democrat.

The click of the doctor's whip, swinging above the horses' heads, was the only sound now in the vast silence of the prairie. Dr. McDermott was considering the advisability of replacing the veterans who had given him such long and valiant service over the years. Their slow speed, which appealed greatly to the engrossed young people at this juncture, aroused only the indignant wrath of the harassed doctor. A Ford, racing along the road at breakneck speed, jumping airily over a mud hole and splashing a stream of the thick black slimy stuff over the slow democrat and its occupants, was the last straw for Dr. McDermott. There and then he vowed to pension the veteran geldings and himself acquire one of those infernal machines that of later years had both tormented and tempted him.

Ever and anon now, Cyril would ride a bit ahead, and as if to perform for the special benefit of the girl, Pat, which was the name of his horse, reared up on his front or hind feet, plunged about and did some reckless bucking, shook himself insolently, and otherwise acted up to the thrilled delight of his admiring audience of one. His motions, however, feazed not the rider, in his firm and graceful seat on the animal's back, holding the peppery young bronco under complete and careless control. The horse, a youngster of five, was impatient at this lagging delay along the trail, and pulled and snorted in an effort to race ahead of the slow plugging veterans.

"Oh, my," said Nettie—he was riding close again—"he's an awful spirited animal, isn't he? Aren't you the least bit afraid?" And then, as he smiled at the idea, she added with the most simple, unfeigned admiration:

"You ride just as if nothing—no kind of a horse—could ever upset you."

His chest swelled with pride, and he beamed upon her.

"'Bout time I knew how to ride. Been ridin' since I was a two-year-'ole."

He offered another sally that brought forth the desired young laughter:

"Say, didn't you notice that I was a bowleg?"

Nettie looked at those brilliantly clad legs—they were clad in orange-coloured fur chaps—and the shape of them was utterly hidden. Their eyes met and they burst out laughing as if they had both heard the funniest joke in the world.

They had turned now into the road allowance which ran directly up to where the log cabin stood on the edge of the land. Something in the stillness, the solitary look of that lone cabin planted on the bare floor of the prairie, sobered them, and they looked at the house with apprehension. Inside, they knew, was an English-woman—a "lady," had said the doctor, and she was very sick.

Silently they dismounted. Dr. McDermott walked ahead of the trio, the cowpuncher leading his horse and keeping close to the girl.

As they stepped into the dim shadows of the bare room, the figure on the hard, homemade bed, tossed itself upward. The face was thin and pinched, with hectic spots of colour on either slightly high cheek-bone; the bright eyes were full of suspicion, and fixed upon them with a sort of fierce challenge. Her hair had been cut to the scalp. Jagged and unlovely it showed up in grotesque tufts, as if trying to push its way out despite the murderous shears. There was that about her crouched-up look against the wall that was curiously like some wild thing at bay.

Nettie's first impulse of shock and fear gave way to one of overwhelming pity as she moved toward the bed. Those bright, defiant eyes met her own, and the woman moistened her dry lips:

"What do you want in my house? Who are you?"

"I'm Nettie Day," said the girl simply, "and I just want to help you."

"I don't want any help," cried the woman violently. "All I want is to be left alone."

The exertion, the violence of her reply, brought on a breathless fit of coughing, and now the woman was too weak to resist the hands that tenderly lifted and held her. When the spasm had passed, she lay inert in Nettie's arms, but when she opened her eyes again, they widened with a strange light. as they stared up fixedly at the pitying face bent over her. The dry lips quivered, something that was pitifully like a smile broke over the sick woman's face. She whispered:

"Why, you look—like—my mother!"

CHAPTER IV

MORE THAN A YEAR HAD PASSED since that day in March when Nettie, the doctor and Cyril Stanley drove along the trail to the cabin on the C.P.R. quarter. Slow but sure changes had taken place upon the land. That sturdy log house that had grown into being represented the efficient labour of young Cyril Stanley's hands. He had built it in the "lay-off time" he had taken that summer. Slowly the holes for the fence posts were going into the ground around the entire quarter. Soon the "home" would be ready for the radiant Nettie. A few more months, and Cyril would leave the Bar Q with sufficient savings to give him and Nettie a start in life.

Things also had moved upon that quarter section where, in defiant solitude, lived the woman who had resented and fought the help forced upon her by the gruff Scotch doctor and Nettie Day.

Her name, it appeared, was Angela Loring, but some wag had named her "Mr." Loring, because of her clipped hair and her working-man's attire, and this name had stuck, though Nettie Day called her "Angel."

Her appearance in Yankee Valley had caused the sensation which always accompanied the arrival of a strange new-comer. There had been the usual tapping of heads and wagging of tongues. The woman was a "bug," pronounced the farm people of Yankee Valley. At all events, she was the kind of "bug" they found it prudent to keep at a safe distance. She had met all overtures of friendship with hostility and contempt. She was on her own land. She desired no commerce with her neighbours. She needed no help. It was nobody's business but her own why she chose to dress and live in this way. That was the substance of her replies to those who ventured to call upon her, and when some jocular fellows pressed their company upon her, she demonstrated her ability to shoot straight—at their feet—so that for a time a joke ran around the country of the number of young "bucks" who limped, and the joshing, jeering taunt: "Mr. Loring will get you if you don't watch out," was the jest of the moment. Thus she became a sort of bugaboo in the popular imagination, but as time passed, the country became used to the woman-hermit and gave her the desired wide berth.

She broke her own land and put in her own crop. She did it inadequately, it is true, but with a certain persistence and intensity which at first amazed and then slowly won the grudging respect and wonder of her neighbours. She had few implements, and these the antiquated tools used by Dr. McDermott when first he had homesteaded in Alberta. Her horses were poor, scrub stock, palmed off upon her by Bull Langdon, who sent them down with the proposition that she could have the four head in exchange for her services on the Bar Q cook car over the haying period on his ranch. Cooks were a rare and precious article in those years, and even a Chinaman was not to be had for love or money. The woman hermit studied the proposition a moment, and then to the surprise of the grinning "hand" who had brought the horses and the offer, she accepted it.

She understood horses well enough, but not the kind used in Alberta for farming purposes.

Her acquaintance had been with the English saddle horses. How could she know the type of draught horse necessary for the plough, the disc, the harrow and the seeder? But she harnessed up the poor stock advanced her by the Bull, obtained her seed by application to the municipality, and her crop went in.

Cutworm ate it to the ground when it had barely shown above the soil.

Grim, and with that distant air of antagonism about her, she went to the Bar Q, and over the haying period she cooked for thirty or forty men. Even then her contact with the crew was a silent one. She cooked and dished up the "grub" and passed it out to them. She had never been known to address a voluntary sentence or question to a soul upon the place, with the single exception of the half-breed Jake, who did her chores and wiped the dishes for her. When Mrs. Langdon made overtures of friendship to her, she curtly told her that she would "quit" if she were "interfered" with. She was in charge of the cook car, and must be left alone.

In the fall, she broke more land, and in the winter she shut herself into her shack, and no one, save Dr. McDermott, who persisted upon calling upon her on his monthly rounds, saw her again till the spring, when she put in a larger crop than the year before.

However, time assuages even if it does not satisfy the hungriest curiosity. In a country like Alberta, even in the present day, we do not scrutinize too closely the history or the past of the stranger in our midst. Alberta is, in a way, a land of sanctuary. Upon its rough bosom, the derelicts of the world, the fugitive, the hunted, the sick and the dying, have sought asylum and cure. The advent of a new-comer, however suspicious or strange, causes only a seven days' wonder and stir. Human nature is, of course, the same the world over, and besides curiosity, surmise, invention, slander, strike forth their filthy fingers to shatter the lives of those we do not know. Fortunately curiosity has a vanishing quality in the ranching country. Time and distance have much to do with this. We cannot shout our gossip of a neighbour across hundreds of miles of territory, and he who toils upon the land from sunrise to sunset may not hustle forth from door to door to bear an evil tale.

There was one, however, in Alberta, who knew somewhat of the history of this strange woman. She had failed to recognize in the country doctor, who stubbornly forced his services and society upon her, the Scotch lad whom twenty-four years before her father had sent away to college in Glasgow.

Dr. McDermott was one of Alberta's pioneer workers. When settlers followed upon the heels of the missionary and the railroads, and planted their rude homestead on the big raw land, Dr. McDermott was there to care for and direct them. He had attended his patients in all parts of the wild country, travelling, in those days, by any and all kinds of primitive vehicle, often afoot, before the roads were staked, when there were no lines of barbed wire fencing to mark the trail, and when a blizzard meant possible blindness or death. He had gone to remote places to bring babies into the world. He had cared for the mother as a physician, and for the help- less households as a mother. He had rolled up his sleeves and cleaned the houses of his patients, he had cooked for them, and washed and cared for and instructed them. He loved the land of his adoption, and knew Alberta as a child knows his mother. He knew that this "last of the big lands," as they called it, was for those who were capable of seizing life with strong, hot hands. It was a hard, a bitter land; a land of toil and struggle, a land of stern and ruthless realities, yet none the less a Land of Romance and of comfort. It possessed the qualities that appealed to a nature such as Angus McDer- mott's. He was grateful to the man who had picked him out from the humble clan of McDermott and had given him the opportunity for an education, so that now he might be of inestimable service to a new race of people—a race of pio- neers and country builders. It was a proud day when, cleared of encumbrances, free of mortgages, taxes paid to date, the land broken and the stout log cabin planted upon it, Angus McDermott deeded the beloved quarter section to the man who had paid for his education.

Now after the passage of the years, the daughter of his benefactor was here upon this bit of Alberta soil. In turn, she was seeking to wrest a living from the land, fighting a desperate fight with poverty, disease and the blows and buffets of the wild new land, which "makes or breaks" a man, as the saying goes in Alberta.

As he drove along the rough roads, chirping absently to the old geldings that plugged slowly along, his mind went back to those sunny days in the old land. Twenty-four years! He rode on and on through the Alberta sunshine, his wide Stetson tilted above a rugged face, whose chief attribute was a quality of sturdy honesty.

CHAPTER V

NETTIE SAT LISTLESSLY on the single step of the Day shack, her hands loosely clasped in her lap. The ripening grain gleamed in the light as golden as her own thick braids. A breeze moved the heavily-laden stalks, till the field seemed to ripple and stir.

This was a crop year, and even upon the rocky land of the "D.D.D." the grain pushed up resistlessly. Nevertheless, looking out upon those waving fields, which represented largely the labour of her own hands and her brothers', Nettie felt no sense of gratification or pride. Her world had suddenly changed and darkened.

The poor, shiftless, happy-go-lucky homesteader of the "D.D.D." had died. Of all that family of twelve, there remained but Nettie. County officials had taken away the younger ones, who were to be "put out" for adoption, while neighbouring farmers had snapped up the growing boys as "likely timber for hard work."

Nettie was alone. She did not know what was to become of her, or whither she would go. She thought vaguely of the great city of Calgary. There she would surely find work; but Nettie was a farm girl, and the city spelled to her mind eternal speed and noise, a feverish, rushing activity which would bewilder and terrify.

She was a silent girl, given to day-dreaming. Humble and simple enough were the dreams of Nettie Day. A clean, small cabin on a quarter section of land; a cow or two; a few pigs; chickens; fields of grain—oats, thick and tall; gleaming, silvery barley; the blue flowering flax; waves of golden wheat. There would be men upon the implements, and herself in a clean kitchen, cooking a meal for the harvest hands, and always her dream embraced within its circle one whose friendly face was tanned and freckled by the sun, whose smile was wide and all-embracing, and who looked at Nettie with eyes that spoke a language that needed no tongue.

"Some day soon," he had said to Nettie, "you and me will be in our own home, girl."

"Soon," to the Scotch-Ontario boy, meant a year or two, or maybe a year or two more than that; when, in fact, the home for Nettie should be snug and complete, and a nest-egg assured in the bank or on the range.

But now everything had changed. The home had been broken up. There was to be an auction of the poor stock upon the place, to raise the price of the mortgage upon the land.

Nettie felt helpless and lost. She missed her father and her little brothers and sisters cruelly, and she dared not think of the baby, so dependent upon her own care. Persistently, her gaze wandered off to the hills, and with a lump in her throat, she looked for Cyril to come.

Unable to read or write, Nettie had, nevertheless, dispatched word to the rider of the Bar Q, through the medium of the half-breed, Jake, who had ridden by on the day after her father's death.

With the noon hour came the farmers and the ranchers, riding in from far and near, for a country auction in Alberta will bring out the people as to a celebration or fair. They came to the Day auction with picnic baskets and hampers, in all kinds of vehicles, democrats, buggies, hay wagons, automobiles, and on horse.

The auctioneer was a little man, with a barking voice. He bustled about the place, appraising the stock and implements, the household effects and furniture. The few head of cattle and horse were driven into a hastily constructed corral of large logs. Bull Langdon held the mortgage upon the "D.D.D." and he expected to have his money back with compound interest.

The sale began at the house, the home-made bits of furniture telling their own tale of the labour of Nettie and her mother. These sold for practically nothing, and some of them created cackles of laughter, as they were shoved out into the jovial circle of farm folk. As bit by bit the familiar pieces were brought from the house and dumped upon the ground for the edification and consideration of the farmers, Nettie, unable to bear the pain of that pitiful sale, sought a refuge in the barn. Here she stood looking down at the fat sow, her father's especial pride and care, and the thirteen little pigs that had come with the spring. Dry sobs wrenched her, and when a Bar Q hand spoke to her, she looked up with her drenched face strangely like that of a wounded child's.

"'Taint no use to cry about nothin'," said Batt Leeson, with pretended roughness. "Them pigs 'll fetch a fancy figger, though five of em's runts."

"I w-wasn't thinkin' of the pigs," said Nettie. "I was w-wondering when Cyril Stanley would come. He's a friend of mine," with a gulp of pride through all her grief.

"Him? Say, he's up at the pure-bred camp at Barstairs. Gittin' the herd in shape for the annual fair circuit. We got the greatest champeen bulls in the world, take it from me. You needn't look for him, girl. He's on his job."

She turned pale at the intelligence, though Cyril had told her of the possibility of his being dispatched to the Bull-camp at Barstairs. It would be impossible for him to come.

With a sick sense of desertion, she returned to where the auction was continuing briskly, and with considerable hilarity. The auctioneer was jumping up and down, as into the circle of log fencing a small bull was being driven.

"Oh, boys!" yelled the auctioneer (a one time showman). "What have we here? This ain't no scrub bull! Betchu he's almost pure Hereford! Betchu he's got a good strain of Bar Q in him! Betchu he's an A 1 calf-thrower. What am I offered? Gentlemen, here's the chance o' your life-time."

A loud laugh burst from the circle of farmers, and Bull Langdon came closer to the fence and squinted appraisingly at the animal.

"Daresay he ain't in prime shape—poor nibblings on the 'D.D.D.' as you' know, gentlemen, but betchu you turn 'im out on some regular grass, he'll turn round and s'prize you. They's the makin's of a smooth bull in that fellow!"

"How old is he?" yelled a wag, making a horn of his hands. "Seems like I seen him at 'D.D.D.' when Dan Day first pulled in."

Before the laughter that swelled up from this sally had half died down, a girl's young savage voice broke upon the gathering. Eyes blazing, breathlessly facing the circle of rough men, Nettie sprang to the defence of the home product.

"It's a lie, Jem Bowers, and you know it! He ain't old. He ain't more than six year old, and he just looks that way— spare and done, 'cause we never had enough feed for our stock. Dad listened to you all and staked his land on this rocky part, while you got the fat places. That bull ain't old, and don't you dare say he is. I guess I ought to know, 'cause I raised him myself from a calf."

A silence greeted this outburst from the girl. Eyes shifted, tongues were stuck into cheeks. Compunction, not unmixed with admiration, showed on the faces of the farmers, aware possibly for the first time of the presence of Nettie, who had kept in the background. Bull Langdon, fists on hips, had moved from his position by the fence, and for the first time, his appraising eye fell fully upon Nettie. He looked the girl over slowly, from head to foot, and as his bold gaze swept her, his eyes slightly bulged and he licked his lips.

Her outburst, probably the only one in all her simple life, had left her flushed and breathless. Her wrath subsiding, she shrank before the united gaze of that crowd of rough men, gathered to buy up their poor possessions. Nettie drew back to the shadow of the house and the sale went on.

Presently it was over. Auctioneer and buyers tramped across the muddy barnyard to the house, there to make a reckoning. As they came to the step, Nettie, her hands spasmodically clasped, met them.

"Is everything—sold?" she asked the auctioneer quaveringly.

"Every last thing upon the place gone under the hammer. Did pretty well I'll say. Not too bad prices."

"Then there'll be something for my brothers and sisters?"

"Not on your life they won't. Scarcely enough to satisfy the mortgage and pay up the debts. You ask Mr. Langdon there. He holds the mortgage, and he's bought in most o' the truck himself."

Nettie turned her head slowly and looked in the face of Bull Langdon. Then her head dropped. The Bull had stepped forward. One big, thick forefinger went up to the auctioneer, as it had risen when he had bought head by head the stock and cattle.

"How about the gell? My wife needs a good, strong gell for the housework, and I'm willin' to take her along with her dad's old truck."

One of the farmer's wives, a pale, anemic creature who had sidled next to Nettie, whispered:

"Don't chu go with him, Nettie. He ain't no good."

As the eyes of the Bull fell upon her, the woman quailed, and she said aloud:

"Mrs. Langdon's the kindest woman in this country. You'd be workin' for a good woman, Nettie. You're a lucky girl to get the chance."

All that Nettie was thinking then was that Cyril Stanley worked for the Bar Q. She would be near Cyril; they would meet, perhaps daily. That thought sent her toward Bull Langdon, with a hopeful look in the eyes raised shyly, if fearfully, toward him.

"I'll go, Mr. Langdon," said Nettie Day. "I got to get a place anyway, and I might as well go along with you."

The Bull withdrew his glance. Finger up again, he summoned his "hands."

"Round up them 'dolgies,' you, Buzz. You, Batt, bring along the pigs in the wagon. Damn you, Block, get them horses back. Where in the h— d'yer think we're rangin'? You Boob, roll off o' your horse there. Saddle that pinto for the gell. Here, tighter on the cinch. Shorten them stirrups. Here, gell!"

His big hand went under her arm, assisting her upon the horse, but it closed and squeezed the soft yielding flesh. Testing the length of the stirrups, he looked up into her face with such an expression, that she was suddenly filled with alarm and terror. As his big hand continued to tug at the stirrup strap, his arm pressed upon her knee. She said hastily:

"Let 'em alone. Them stirrups is all right. I like 'em long."

She shoved her foot into the leather thong. Slapping the horse across the neck with the reins, she urged it along. She had a sudden impulse to flee, though from what, she could not have said. She was possessed with an imperative urge to leave far behind her the huge cowman, with his wild, possessive eyes.

She went along the trail at a breathless gallop, and it was only when his hand reached across the neck of her horse and planted itself upon the pummel of her saddle, she realized that he had never left her side.

"Hi, there, you don't want to run as a starter. Take it easy."

On and on they went, across country, past the wide-spreading pastures and grain fields, odorous with the bumper crop which that year was to put Alberta on the grain map of the world, past the homely little log cabin that Cyril had built for Nettie, and past the quarter where the cropped-haired woman lived in hermit-like seclusion. On and on, till they came to ever higher grades, and climbed upward toward the hill country.

Facing them, under a sunset that spread in a glow of red and gold that embraced all of the heavens, the mighty Rocky Mountains rose like a great dream before them. Into the sunset rode the girl and the man, while the perfect stillness of the Alberta evening closed in about them, and she lost herself in her old aspirations, with the nearness of the long yearned-for hills. Thoughts of Cyril, sweet and wistful, interposed to calm and reassure her. The man riding beside her was forgotten; forgotten everything but the spell of the Alberta twilight, and the dear thoughts of her love.

At last they were before one of those great Alberta ranch gates, its rails of logs ten feet long. The Bull had alighted, had opened the gate. Now they were cantering up the hill.

In Alberta, the sunlight lingers until late into the night, and a mellow glow suffuses the land, gilding the meanest spot, and turning the country into dim oceans and mountains of beauty. Under this light, the white and green ranch buildings of the Bar Q shone up like a small city planted upon a hill top. This first sight of the great Bar Q caused the girl from the Dan Day Dump to catch her breath in awe and admiration.

The Bull had dismounted, and Nettie, with his hand under her arm, had come also to the ground; but the arm stayed about her possessively, and she was pulled closely to the cowman. She stared, fascinated, into the face so close to her own.

"That Pinto's yours, gell," said Bull Langdon, "and if you're the right kind of a gell, and treat the Bull right, it's the first o' the presents you'll be gettin'."

Nettie shrank back, but she tried valiantly to hide her feelings of fear and repulsion. She said breathlessly:

"I don't want nothing that I don't earn."

At that the Bull laughed—a big, hoarse chuckle.

"You'll get all that's comin' to you, gell," he said.

CHAPTER VI

LIFE WAS PLEASANT FOR NETTIE DAY AT THE BAR Q. Dressed in pink and white gingham house dresses, supplied by Mrs. Langdon, she seemed to grow prettier with every day.

The big, clean ranch house, shining with sunlight and space, was a revelation to the girl who had lived all her life in the two rooms of the poor shack, with her parents and her nine little brothers and sisters.

It flattered the vanity of Bull Langdon to have a "show place" on the Banff National Highway. He had built the main ranch house upon the crest of a hill that commanded the road to Banff, and the widespreading buildings, ornate in design and paint, were placed with a view to showing up well from the road, so that all who travelled along the highway would slow up for a view of the Bar Q.

Nettie's advent was both a surprise and a joy to the wife of the cattleman, who took a childish pride in at last "keeping a girl."

For a number of years, the Bar Q had maintained a cook car, whither the "hands" went for "grub." It was on some such vehicle that Angela Loring had served. Now a thin and musty-smelling Chinaman dominated the car. It was a shrinking, silent figure, who banged down the chow before the men, and paid no heed to protest or squabble. In winter, the Chinaman was moved to the pure-bred Bull camp at Barstairs, and the men left at the foothill ranch "batched" in the bunk-houses.

Though the main cooking was done on the cook car, there yet remained an enormous amount of work at the ranch house, for besides the housework, the bread and butter for the ranch were made there by Mrs. Langdon. She "put down" the pork in brine, cured and smoked it; she made hundreds of pounds of lard, sausage meat, headcheese, corned beef and other meat products. She made the soap, cared for the poultry and vegetable garden, and she canned quantities of fruit and vegetables for the winter months. She was always working, always running hither and thither about the house, hurrying to "have things ready," for her husband had a greedy appetite, and her mind revolved about ways and means of propitiating and appeasing him.

During the latter years, however, her health had been visibly failing. The long years of hard work, the yearly birth of the dead baby, life and association with the overbearing cattleman, were taking their toll and sapping the strength of the wife of Bull Langdon.

Bull was what was known in the cattle world as a "night rider." In the earlier days, it was said that he did all of his "dirty work" at night. Bunches of cattle were then moved and driven under the silence and shelter of the night. Rivalry and strife and bitter enmity is a peculiarity of the cattle country, and the Bull wreaked his vindictive spite upon his neighbours in the night. Then their herds were slipped out of pastures and corrals, and driven over the tops of canyon and precipice. That, however, was of the past. The cowman was cautious now that he had arrived at a place of security and power. Rustling and stealing were dangerous undertakings in these days when trails had turned into highways, and small ranches were beginning to dot the edges of the range.

Howbeit, night riding had become more or less of a habit with the man, and this habit was one that took a hard toll from the wife who waited up for his return, with the supper always propitiatingly set before him.

In the latter years, premonitions of the breaking of her strength had been ominously evident to Mrs. Langdon, but against the "thought" of ill health she persistently fought. She had an ingenuous faith which she had imbibed from tracts and books that had drifted into her hands from her teaching days. She denied the existence of evil or illness in the world, and when it pushed its ugly fist into her face, or wracked her frail body, she bravely recited over and over again like an incantation a little formula in which she asserted that her pain was an error; that she was in the best of health, and that everything in the world was good and beautiful, and in the image of God. Whether she deluded herself or not, it is certain that this desperate philosophy, if such it could be called, was the crutch that upheld her and kept her from insanity over the turbulent years of her life with Bull Langdon, and left her still with her faith in mankind, and singularly innocent of wrong.

Nettie's coming, therefore, was hailed as a "demonstration" of her faith. The strong, willing, cheerful girl was welcomed with a grateful heart and open arms.

It was pleasant, for a change, to take things easily; to have all the heavier work done by the big, competent girl. Better than the relief from the hard labour, was the companionship of another woman in the ranch house. Only a woman who has been isolated long from her own sex can appreciate what it means when another woman comes into her life.

Nettie would place a rocking-chair for her mistress on the back veranda, bring the basket of mending, and with her slow, shy smile, say:

"Now, Mrs. Langdon, you fall to on them socks and leave me to do the work."

Mrs. Langdon would consent when Nettie could bring her work also to the veranda, and as the one sewed or crocheted, the other churned and worked the butter, kneaded the bread or prepared the vegetables for the day. Work thus became a pleasure, and the light voice of her mistress chattering of many happy topics, made a pleasant accompaniment to their work. If Nettie returned indoors, Mrs. Langdon soon followed her. She took a pride in teaching the girl her own special recipes, and they would both laugh and explain over the mistakes or success of the eager-to-learn Nettie.

Slowly, between the two women, something more than mere friendship grew into being.

Although it was against the rules for the Bar Q "hands" to come to the ranch house, save when summoned by the Bull, or on an especial errand, Nettie's presence there was widely known and commented upon, and many were the ingenious devices invented by the men to obtain a sight or a word with the girl. Bull, however, was more than ever on the watch for an infraction of this rule, and more than one employé was "fired" for loitering in the neighbourhood of the ranch house, or suffered the indignity and pain of a blow from the heavy hand of the boss. However, harvest had set in on the prairie, where Bull Langdon had a great grain ranch. Thither the owner of the Bar Q departed to superintend the harvesting operations.

In spite of Bull Langdon, Cyril and Nettie were not long in devising a means of meeting.

Nettie would slip from the house after supper, and Mrs. Langdon would go early to bed, as was the farm custom. There was a brief field between the house and a clump of willows, behind which was a deep coulie, where the wild-raspberries and gooseberries grew in profusion. Here, hidden by the thick growth, Nettie would pick berries, stopping ever and anon to listen for a sound that only she and Cyril understood—the long-drawn whistle that was like the note of an oriole. At the sound of that musical note, Nettie would stop picking, and, with parted lips, shining eyes and beating heart, she would wait for her lover to come to her in the deep bush.

This was the season when the daylight lingered far into the night, when the soft light of the night sun upon the still and sleeping land bathed everything in a romantic glow. In this glow, young Cyril and Nettie would sit on a knoll, with the berry bushes on all sides and above and below them, and "hold hands," thrilling at the touch of each other, and murmur their joyful confidence and hopes.

Cyril was what the country folk would have described as "slow" with girls, and Nettie was innocent. She had had no companions of her own age. She knew not what it was to have a girl friend. Cyril was her first "beau." This simple "holding of hands" constituted a deep happiness, an exciting adventure that made them tremble with a vague longing for something more. Cyril had the clumsy shyness of the country boy who has known no women. It was two weeks before he found the courage and power to place his arm clumsily about the girl's waist. That progress, daring and full of an exciting joy, was the prelude to something he had not calculated upon. The close pressure of the girl's warm young body against his, the automatic lifting of her face, as it almost touched his own, brought the inevitable consequence. For the first time in either of their lives, they kissed. They lost themselves in that single, ever closer kiss. Time and place, thought of all else on earth, disappeared from their minds. Close clasped together, there in the deep berry bushes, they clung ecstatically together.

Upon their blissful dream a harsh voice grated and broke. Even as they drew apart, their eyes heavy and warm with this new rapture they had just discovered, they dimly recognized the voice of Bull Langdon. From somewhere in the direction of the corrals he was roaring for his "hands." They could hear his cursing demands. He must have ridden up soundlessly, and, peeved at finding no one about the place, was venting his temper in this fashion.

"Oh, my!" murmured Nettie, half drawing from his arms and half unconsciously leaning to him. "He'll be wantin' you, Cyril."

"Let'm want," said the boy, hungry again to feel the touch of those warm lips upon his own. "I'm not workin' nights for no man, and if he ain't satisfied, I guess I can quit any old time now. You say the word when, Nettie. I'm ready for you, girl. And, Nettie—give us another kiss, will you?"

"Cyril, I got to get to the house. Mrs. Langdon's gone to bed, and he'll be looking for something to eat, and it's not her place to get it for him, when I'm here to do the work."

"You won't have to work for no one but me soon, Nettie. I'll take care of you for the rest of your days. Nettie, I never kissed a girl before. That is true as God."

"Neither did I—never kissed a fellow."

"Kiss me again, then."

Only for a moment she remained in his arms this time, for somewhere, close at hand now, the demanding voice of Bull Langdon was heard, his words causing Nettie to break away with dismay.

"Where's that gell? Why ain't she on her job?"

Nettie clambered up the slope of the coulie and went running across the grass to the house. As she paused at the wide-open door, her basket still on her arm, Bull Langdon, now in his seat, his legs outspread before him, moved around to stare at her, his wild, covetous glance, as always, holding her fascinated and breathless with a vague fear.

"Where've we been at this early hour of the night?"

"I have been picking berries," faltered Nettie, trying vainly to steady her voice.

"Oh, you have, heh?"

Her cheeks were redder than any berries that ever grew, and her eyes shone star-bright. Her white bosom rose and fell, partly from the thrill of her late adventure, and partly from the suddenly interposing fear.

"Pickin' berries in the night, heh? You're smart, ain't you?"

"Oh, yes, it was light as day, you see, and I don't mind—"

"Let's see what you got."

He reached out, seemingly for the basket, but his hand closed upon hers about the handle. There he gripped tightly, while with his other hand, he swept up the cover and peered into the empty basket.

"Let go my hand!" she cried in a stifled voice. "You're hurtin' me!"

For answer he possessed himself of the other, and steadily drew her nearer and nearer to him. She struggled and twisted about, suppressing her inclination to scream, for fear that her mistress might hear. But, in fact, it was the clip-clop of her mistress's loose bedroom slippers on the stairs that caused her release.

Mrs. Langdon, her hair in paper curls, and with a grey flannelette kimono thrown over her night-dress, hurried down the stairs.

"Oh, Bill"—she was the only person who never called him "Bull"—"is it you? Are you back? I'm so sorry I didn't hear you get in or I'd a been down at once. We'll have something ready for you in a minute. Nettie, bring some of that fresh headcheese, and cut it from the new bowl, mind you, and maybe Mr. Langdon'll like something to drink, too. You made butter to-day, didn't you? Well, bring some fresh buttermilk, or maybe you'd like something hot to drink. Which'd you have, Bill?"

He never replied to her many light questions, and she never expected him to. She nodded and smiled to the girl, and Nettie hurried to the pantry. Mrs. Langdon fluttered about her husband, helping him to remove his heavy riding boots and coat, and putting away his hat and gauntlets. He endured her ministrations, but in spite of her chatter and numerous questions, he remained silent. When Nettie brought the tray with its fresh home-made headcheese, thick layer cake and buttermilk, he drew up before it and ate in a sort of absorbed silence.

"Will you be wanting me any more tonight, Mrs. Langdon?" asked Nettie.

"No, Nettie, thank you. Run along to bed. If Mr. Langdon needs anything else, I'll get it. Good-night, dear."

Bull, having finished the last of the food before him, reached for his boots and began again to pull them on.

"Oh, Bill, you're not going out again, are you?" exclaimed Mrs. Langdon, with nervous anxiety.

He tightened his belt without speaking, his big chest swelling under his moose-hide shirt. Spurs rattling, he tramped across the room and out into the yard.

At the bunkhouse lights were out, and all hands save one abed. Cyril sat on the edge of his bunk, still dressed, chin cupped in his hands, as he gave himself up to his dreams.

The great bulk of the cattleman filled the doorway. His forefinger up, he singled out Cyril. The young man stood up, and with a glance back at his sleeping mates, he joined his employer outside the bunkhouse.

Fists on hips, an attitude characteristic of the Bull, he scrutinized in the now steadily deepening dusk of the night the young fellow sturdily and coolly facing him, apparently unmoved and unafraid.

"Want chu to be ready first thing in the morning to ride over to Barstairs. Want chu to get them bulls in shape for the circuit. Goin' to exhibit in St. Louis, Kansas City, Chicago, San Francisco and other cities in the States. You do well by the bunch here, and there's a bonus on your pay, and you go along with the herd to the U.S."

Aforetime, this unexpected promotion would have elated Cyril. Now, in spite of his astonishment, he hesitated, and in his slow Scotch way he turned the matter over in his mind. After a moment:

"I don't know as I want the job, boss. Fact is, I'm thinkin' of quittin'. Thinkin' o' goin' on my own."

"On your own! You ain't got nothin' to go on your own with."

"I got my homestead. House's built, land partly fenced. I traded in my cattle for implements, and I got six head of horse left, and that's not too bad as a starter."

"How far d'you think you can git on that much, unless you got a stake behind you?"

The young man weighed the question thoughtfully and carefully. A bit sadly he replied:

"Not very far, but it'll do as a starter, and next year—"

"Next year ain't here yet. Besides, it depends on what you're countin' on. You aimin' to get married?"

Somehow the question infuriated the Bull, so that he shot it at the boy, despite the effort at self-control, and his eyes blazed through the darkness. But Cyril was too absorbed by his own dreams to note the Bull's voice or attitude. After a pause, he answered slowly:

"Yep."

"You can't raise no family on what you got now," said the Bull hoarsely. "Things ain't the same as when I started in. You better wait a year or two. Take on this proposition I'm offerin' you, and you'll be in better shape to do the right thing by the gell you marry then. There's a ten dollar a month raise for you, and a bonus of a hundred at the end of the season."

A long pause, as this sank into Cyril, and he slowly weighed the matter in his mind. A few months more or less would matter little to him and Nettie. The money would mean a lot. There were certain articles he had set his heart on buying for Nettie for the house. Household utensils, which a country travelling salesman, who had put up over night at the Bar Q, had shown him enticing samples of. After awhile, with decision:

"Maybe you're right, boss. I'm on. Barstairs, eh? I'll be on the job first thing in the morning."

But when he rode out in the quiet dawn, with no one but Jake to bid him good-bye, Cyril's heart was full, and as he went by the ranch house, his glance sought Nettie's window, in the vain hope that she might by some chance be up and in sight. Jake had a message for her, and he felt sure that she would understand. It was a common occurrence to dispatch riders on trips such as this, and Cyril was of a race that put his duty before his pleasure. Far-sighted and canny, he was prepared to serve and wait an extra year, if need be, for the girl he loved.

At the thought of that future, shared with Nettie, his heart lifted. The greyness of the approaching dawn slowly softened, and the miracle of the sunrise broke over the sleeping land. Far and wide on all sides stretched an incomparable sky, a shadowy, gilded loveliness, as if a misty veil were slowly being lifted, and there stepped into full bloom the marvellous sunglow of Alberta. His spirits rose with the sunlight, and as his horse loped along the trail to Barstairs, Cyril Stanley lifted his young voice in song.

CHAPTER VII

THE DAYS WERE GETTING LONGER. The fall round-up was under way, and the Bull rode the range with his men. For a week, long files of cattle had been pouring down from the hills, to meet in the lower pastures and automatically form into that symmetrical army that moved moaning low before the drivers, to the corrals and pens where they were sorted over and separated.

It was a torture period for the cattle, for the Bar Q branded, dehorned and weaned in the early fall. Day and night the incessant bawling of over two thousand calves and outraged mothers, penned in separate fields or corrals, rent the air.

The round-up was an early and swift one this year, for Bull Langdon was due to leave for the States with his pure-bred bulls in early November. He seemed possessed of indefatigable energy and vitality, and no amount of riding seemed to affect him. It was no uncommon thing for him after a night and day of riding, to bring up finally at the ranch house at midnight and sit down to the big meal prepared by the girl, summoned by a thump upon her door. Little conversation passed between them at these times, but once when the cattleman had volunteered the information that they were about through, Nettie said, with apparent relief:

"Then there will be no more branding. I'm glad of that."

The cattleman leaned across the table, his elbows upon it and a knife and fork in either hand. His meaning glance pinned the girl fairly.

"One more head," he said. "I'll put my personal brand upon that maverick before I go."

The following day she was dispatched to Morley, an Indian Trading Post, which was the nearest post office, after the Bar Q mail. It was eight miles from the ranch, and Nettie went on horseback, returning in about two and a half hours, in time to get the supper.

There was no one about the place when she rode into the corrals. Dismounting, she unsaddled her horse, hung bridle and saddle in the barn, and let the horse out to pasture. Hurrying to the house, she found the big kitchen deserted. Usually upon her return from such a message, Mrs. Langdon was accustomed to prepare the supper. Supposing her mistress was taking her afternoon nap, Nettie went about the preparation of the supper. She peeled her potatoes and set them on the range, quickly beat up a pan full of buttermilk biscuits and put them in the oven. The table set, she sliced the cold meat, and put the kettle on for tea.

By this time, there being still no sign of Mrs. Langdon, she ran upstairs and tapped upon her door. There was no reply. Nettie opened the door and looked in. The room was empty, and the wide open closet door revealed the fact that it had been stripped.

A feeling of alarm and encroaching fear for a moment swept her. She ran breathlessly down the stairs and out into the barnyard. Not a hand was about, though far across the pastures, she could see the fence riders riding toward the south, their day's work done. Jake, driving in the milk cows, came over the crest of the hill, and slowly loped down to the barnyard, stopping to water his horse. He did not see Nettie at first waiting for him at the cowshed, and when he did, began to jabber while still on horse. One by one the cows went into their stalls, and stood, bags full, patiently waiting to be milked. Jake, full of his news, dismounted. He had a pronounced impediment in his speech, and when excited, could barely bring the words out intelligently.

"Mis' Langdon—her gone off—off—off." He pointed vividly toward the mountains. "Rode on nortermobile to a station. Goin' far away on train—Choo-choo-choo."

Nettie stared at him blankly. She could barely comprehend the bald fact that her mistress was gone, and in her anxiety she plied the boy with questions.

Where had she gone? When? Who had gone with her? Why did she go? What had she taken? How long was she to be gone?

As, breathlessly, she shook the ragged sleeve of the breed in her impatience to make him understand her, the honk of an automobile horn caused her to look toward the garage, into which the Bull was backing. She hurried across the barnyard, her fear of the man forgotten in her intense anxiety about her mistress.

Fists on hips, in his characteristic pose, at the wide door of the garage, he awaited her approach.

"Is—is it true that Mrs. Langdon has gone away?"

"Yep. Just taken her to the station. Gone up to Banff."

"Banff! Will she be gone for long?"

She hardly realized that her lips were quivering and that her eyes were full of tears.

The soft golden sunset was on all sides of them, and the brooding hush of the ending day lent a beauty and stillness to the evening that was full of poetry; but the man, with his calculating, bulging eye, saw nothing but her softly maturing beauty, the rounded curve of her bosom, the whiteness and softness of her neck, the rose that came and went in her cheeks, the scarlet lips, that aroused in his breast a tormenting passion such as he had never experienced for any woman before.

Nettie repeated her question, her voice catching in the sob that would come despite her best efforts. With the going of both Cyril and her mistress, she felt deserted and even desperate.

"Will she be gone long, I asked you?"

"Long enough to suit me," said the Bull slowly. "She's took a holiday. Guess she's entitled to one, now we've got a gell like you to take her place up to the house. I'm thinkin' you'll fill the bill fine and suit me down to a double T. Is supper ready?"

She stared up at him through the haze before her eyes, piteously, her lips moving, almost as if in entreaty. She tried to say:

"It'll be on the table in a few minutes," but the words were blubbered through the tears which began to fall heavily now in spite of her. Blindly she moved toward the house, holding her apron to her face. Absorbed in her grief, she was unconscious of the fact that the Bull pressed closely to her side, and that it was his big hand, under her arm, that guided her to the house. Inside the kitchen, he held her for a space, as she gasped and cried.

"I won't stay here alone."

"Yer don't have to, gell," said the Bull huskily. "I'm here."

"You!"

She wrenched her arm free.

"I'm not going to stay in this house alone with *you!*" she cried.

"Ain't you? Mebbe you'd prefer the bunkhouse then?"

The Bull was chuckling coarsely.

"I won't stay nowhere at Bar Q. I'm goin' to get out—to-night."

"As you say, gell. I told the wife not to set too much store by you, but no, she'd have her way. Said you could take her place and do the work fine, and she thought she could do as the doctor said, and git away for a change."

Nettie paused, the thought of her mistress's confidence in her holding her in her headlong purpose to escape.

"So I could do the work alone. It's not that. It's just that— that I'm afraid to be here alone—with you," she blurted out.

"Far's that goes, I'm hikin' for Barstairs myself to-night. Goin' on up to the Bull camp. We're leavin' for the States shortly, and I got to go along."

Something was burning on the stove, and she rushed to lift the potatoes. The Bull had seated himself at the table, and was buttering a chunk of bread. Nettie hesitated a moment, and then as the man, apparently oblivious and indifferent to her presence, continued to munch in abstracted silence, Nettie took her place at the table. She poured the tea and passed his cup to him and helped herself to a piece of the cold roast pork. The potato dish was on his left side, and after a moment, she timidly asked him to pass it to her. He shoved the dish across without looking up, and continued to pack down—an expression of his own—the food.

The meal finished in strange silence; she cleared the table and washed the dishes, meanwhile electrically aware of every move of the man about the big room. He had taken down his sheepskin riding-coat and had pushed his legs into fur chaps. There was the jingle of the spurs as they were snapped on to his heels. He took down the quirt and huge hat hanging to a deer head's horns, clapped the latter upon his head, and tramped to the door. All of his preparations had been for a long ride. At the door he threw back an order to her:

"Anyone telephones, I'll reach Barstairs by six or seven in the morning. They can get me there. Have Jake at the house for chores. Let 'im sleep off the kitchen."

She nodded dumbly, conscious only of a vast sense of relief. He was gone.

CHAPTER VIII

NEVER HAD THE RANCH HOUSE SEEMED SO LARGE or so empty. An overwhelming sense of homesickness swept the lonely girl, an appalling longing to again see and be with her little brothers and sisters, now so widely scattered about the country.

The days were gradually becoming shorter, and with the vanishing of the light about ten, a still darkness closed in upon the hill country. If the days were sun-freighted, the nights were still and almost bleak.

Nettie Day knelt by her window. She could see the lights in the row of bunkhouses, and someone was moving about the corrals with a lantern in his hands. For how long she knelt by the window she could not have said, but she felt no inclination for sleep, and put off preparing for bed as long as possible.

The vast silence of the hills seemed to press down about the place, and in the utter stillness of the night the low wailing of a hungry coyote in the hills awakened weird echoes. A healthy, calm-natured girl, Nettie knew not what the meaning of nerves might be. Nevertheless, she experienced a psychic premonition of disaster on that night, and when the depression pressed down unbearably upon her, she could not resist calling to Jake from her window.

Stick on shoulder, the breed came from the kitchen door and grinned up at her in the dusk. Jake was in one of his periods of delusion, and, as sentry before an Indian war camp, he patrolled fearlessly, but with catlike caution. His mere presence, however, comforted her, but her cheek blanched when the breed, returned to the house, let out a startled cry—the cry of one suddenly struck down. She said to herself:

"Jake's playing! I guess he's shooting at himself with his old arrows. My, he's a queer one!"

Long since the lights at the bunkhouses had twinkled out, and the men had "turned in." The "hands" of the Bar Q were early risers, and "hit the bunks" with the departing day.

The last sign of life had vanished. Even the coyote was silent, and the darkness deepened.

Nettie turned from her window at last. Her long plaits of hair hung down, like a Marguerite's, on either side of her shoulder. In her white night-dress, she looked touchingly virginal and sweet. Her hands uplifted, she started to coil the braids, when something—a stealthy, careful motion—caused her to pause. She stood still in the middle of the room, her eyes wide and startled, staring at that door.

There was a lamp on her bureau, and the bureau was by the door. Slowly the knob turned, and she felt the push against the frail door, which she had, however, locked.

Almost paralysed with fear, she nevertheless seized the solitary chair in the room and thrust its back under the door-knob, so that its two back feet tight on the floor made a leverage and barricade against the now loudly crunching wood. She blew out the light and retreated toward the window.

There was a sound of rending steel, and the lock crashed through. The upturned chair quivered on its two back feet, held sturdily in place a moment and then splintered under the iron strength of the man without.

As the door gave way, she lost her senses, and unable to move, like some fascinated thing, she watched the approach of the Bull. She knew that she was trapped, and, hands at her throat, she tried to force to her lips the cry that would not come.

She was in a black dream, a merciless nightmare.

She awoke screaming wildly:

"Cyril, Cyril, Cyril! Cyril! Cyril!" and over and over again, "Cyril!"

Like one gone stark mad, she groped her way to the window and threw herself out.

When she came to consciousness, the bright, hard sun was in her eyes. She stared up at the brilliant blue sky. Jake knelt on the grass beside her, and he tried to move her to the shadow of the house. She moaned:

"Leave me be, I want to die."

Jake muttered excitedly.

"Him! Him! Him see—him hurt Nettie. Last night him hurt Jake bad."

"Him!" She knew whom Jake meant by "him," and threw up her arm as if to shield herself from a blow. The shadow of the Bull was cast above her, and she cowered and cringed from it.

"How'd you git here?" He looked up at the window. "You got to cut out this damn nonsense. I ain't aimin' to hurt you, but you can't lay out here. Here, I'll carry you into the house. Keep still, will yer? D'you want me to tie you?"

Her struggles ceased. Eyes closed, she submitted limply, as he lifted her in his arms and carried her to the house. Jake followed, wringing his hands and whimpering like a dog.

On the fourth day, holding to the banisters, she managed to limp downstairs. For a long time she sat on the hard kitchen chair, staring unseeingly before her. Even when she heard the heavy tramp of the Bull's feet on the outside porch, she did not raise her head, and as he came in, her hopeless gaze still remained on space before her.

"Hello! Whatchu doin' down here? How'd you get down here?"

"I came down myself," said Nettie listlessly. "My ankle ain't hurtin' me no more."

"I'd-a-carried you down if you'd asked me," he grunted angrily. "I done everything a man could for a girl. Who's been waitin' on you hand and foot these last four days, just as if you was a delicate lady, instead of a hired girl on a ranch? What more d'you want? The more you do for some folks, the more they want."

Nettie said nothing, but two big tears suddenly rose out of her eyes and splashed slowly down her cheeks. She resented these tears—a sign of weakness, where she felt hard and frozen within, and she peevishly brushed them away.

"What you cryin' about?"

"I jus' want that you should let me alone," said Nettie.

"You'll be let alone soon enough now. I got to go to Barstairs, and I got to go on to the States. We're billed up at the fairs over there, and I got to go along with my bulls. I'd take you with me, if it wasn't for that young buck at Barstairs. I ain't plannin' on sharing you with no one, do you get me? You belong to Bull Langdon. I got you at the sale, same as I got the rest of your dad's old truck, and what the Bull gets his hands on he keeps. It's up to yourself how you get treated. I'm free-handed with them that treats me right. My old woman ain't strong. She'll croak one of these days, and 'twon't be long before they'll be another Mrs. Langdon at Bar Q. You treat the Bull right, and you'll be the second Mrs. Langdon."

Nettie twisted her hands in her apron. Her heart ached dully, and at the mention of her mistress's name a fierce lump rose persistently in her throat.

"Well, what you got to say to that?"

She did not answer, and he pursued wrathfully:

"You're sulking now, and you're sore on me, but you'll get over that, gell. I'll knock it out of your system damn soon, if you don't, and you'll find out that it will pay you to be on the right side of the Bull rather than the wrong."

"I ain't going to make you mad," said Nettie piteously, shrinking under the implied threat of his approach and words. He chuckled, pleased with his power.

"Well, I'll be off. If it weren't for them bulls, nothing would take me from you now, gell, but I ain't fool enough to neglect my *bulls* for a gell. I'm goin' along with the herd far as St. Louis, and I'll be back to you before the month is out."

His big lips closed over hers. She felt strangled in a loathsome embrace. Once again she was alone.

She sat in the kitchen for more than an hour after the departure of the Bull, still in that attitude of stupefied apathy. Then she limped upstairs, went into her room, closed the battered door, and sat down on the side of her bed, holding her head in her hands. She had no feeling save one of intense weariness and dead despair. Presently, still dressed, she fell sideways on the bed. She slept the long, unbroken sleep of one mentally and physically exhausted.

CHAPTER IX

(Part of Journal kept by Lady Angela Loring.)

I HATE MEN AND I DESPISE WOMEN. I am afraid of children. Animals are my only friends.

They call me the "old man-maid recluse, on the edge of Yankee Valley." I have heard them refer to me as "that tough old nut." They grin in my face, but they keep at a respectable distance from me, which, so far as I am concerned, is desirable. Most people have the souls of coyotes. They circle about you, with snarling mouths, if you evince fear of them, but they scatter and whine and hide, when you show fight.

It is not of any consequence to me what my neighbours, or, as far as that goes, anyone in the world thinks of me, or what they call me. I suffer no pang from the knowledge of the fact that my face is hard and toughened by work and the weather, and by other things that I need not mention here. I have no hair even on my head—that is, none to speak of, for I deliberately cut my hair to the scalp, and I am not going to let it grow again. It's cool and comfortable this way and it suits my purpose. My hands are as hard as my face. I wear men's clothes, not because I admire anything about the mean race of men, against whom, in fact, I feel a deep-rooted aversion, but because it is a more practical and comfortable mode of dress, and because I wish to forget that I am a woman.

Nothing can undo the past. That is a tight, relentless knot that even the hand of God may not unravel.

Some people find a cure for their hurts and ills in a contemplation of griefs greater than their own. For my part, I believe it is easier to carry one's own burdens rather than those of one we love. Men have jilted women before my time. I could have survived that outrage and humiliation. From somewhere within me, I would have found the courage and the strength to face the disillusionment and shock; but the destruction of my father was the unendurable tragedy that embittered my whole life. The man I was to have married, and whom my father trusted, not only cheated and robbed us, but was as certainly my father's murderer as if he had stabbed him to the heart.

Even after the passage of the days, the weeks and the years—yes, and the little minutes and hours that have ticked off the aching period of my pain, I find I cannot set down on cold white paper that which befell. I seem to suffer from inner fractures that not even the balm of time can heal.

Certain memories pursue us like malignant shadows that are a part of our very selves. We cannot escape them, lest we cut down our own lives. So I will write of other things. I will write of that which now absorbs me; of that which, in a way, has given me a purpose in life. My ranch! This bit of Alberta soil. Strange, that I should have first learned of its existence at a time when I believed that life was ended for me; for an eminent physician had actually pronounced my death sentence.

He gave me but a few months only in which to live. I did not wish to die. I had a reason for living. I was consumed with the desire of accomplishing my vengeance upon him whom I held responsible for my father's death and my own torment. That sounds melodramatic, and I suppose if I had a sweet disposition I would bear in mind that revenge is sweet only for God. But my nature is not sweet, and hell raged within me. It was strange, as I have said, at that time suddenly to learn of the existence of this ranch. I seemed to see it in a dream—far off under a spotlight of Alberta sunlight. A hypnotist sometimes magnetizes his subject with a piece of glass. It wavers back and forth before his staring gaze, till, unconsciously, against his will even, he is drawn by its spell. I was drawn clear across the ocean by the magnet of my ranch. I experienced a fundamental revolution of character, and a titanic and even heroic inner battle stirred within me. I felt a strange excitement, a new interest, and I said to myself:

"It is there I will go! It is there I will hide myself. I will bury my old pains and wounds! I will begin life again! I will not die! By my will I will conquer all of the ills of this poor, diseased body of mine."

And so I came to Alberta. With these two hands of mine—so soft and useless in the old land—I have cleaved out my own salvation. That is a strange way to put it; yet I believe that my physical toil has been the main factor in giving me back the life which the English physician declared was practically over.

I broke my own land. I put in my own crop. I have hayed and fenced and chored. I have drudged in the house, and upon the land. I made my own furniture, and I practically rebuilt the shack.

"Necessity is the mother of invention," goes the proverb, though I loathe proverbs. One can find an opposing one for even the best of them. Some people pin proverbs and poems and texts and stupid platitudes upon their souls as on their walls. I suppose they get a sort of comfort and help from them, such as a crutch affords to a cripple, and few there be in life who can walk without a mental crutch. I never saw a human being yet who did not at least mentally limp....

My ranch lies midway between the good grain lands on one side and the hill country on the other. To farm is to gamble on the largest scale possible; for the earth may be said to be our board, the seed our dice and the elements, the soil, the parasites, the hail, the frost, the rust and the drought, these are the cards stacked against us. But, like all gamblers, we are reaching out for a prize that enthrals and lures us, that "pot of gold at the end of our rainbow" is the harvest—the wonderful, glorious, golden harvest of Alberta. Some day it will come to me also.

In the spring, our land is excessively fragrant. The black, loamy soil fairly calls to one to lay the seed within its fertile bosom. Anything will grow in Alberta. It's a thrilling sight to see the grain prick up sturdy and strong. When first my own showed its green head above the earth, I suffered such exhilaration that I could have thrown myself upon the ground and kissed the good old mother earth. Those tiny points of green, there on the soil that I myself had ploughed, disced, harrowed and seeded. I suffered the exquisite pang of the creator.

If only one might shut one's memories up in a box, close tight the lid and turn the key upon them. If but the past could be blotted out, as are our sins by death; then, methinks, we could find comfort and compensation in this poor life once again.

The last generation of the Lorings were a soft-handed, dependent race. I come of an older, a primitive breed. I am a reversion to type, for I love to labour with my hands. Had I been a man I might have been a ditch or a grave digger. I love the earth. When I die I do not want to be cremated. I want to go back to the soil.

Life has not been easy for me in Alberta. Far from it. I might liken my life in this country to a battle, stubborn and never ceasing, yet exhilarating and worth while. My antagonists have been poverty, sickness, cold, and these have driven me to the wall. I have been thwarted, besieged and trapped, but I have known the glorious throb of victory. I face the world, covered with many wounds, but I know that I have won out!

Cutworm took my first crop. Frost destroyed my grain in the second year when it had attained almost full growth. This is all part of the game, of course, and I have turned my sod over and broken more land for the next year's crop.

The hardest part has been my enforced work at the Bar Q. Not the labouring part. I do not mind cooking. There are worse things in the world than that; but one feels muddied by even distant association with a wild brute like Bull Langdon. For him I feel an intuitive and instinctive antipathy. Yet I am not afraid of Bull Langdon. On the contrary Bull Langdon fears me. He never shouts at me. He blusters, and his blood-shot roving eyes fall before mine. He may be the great boss and bully of the Bar Q. With his big bull whip in hand, his cattle may huddle before him, and his men quail and slink away; his wife and the half-breed Jake may tremble, at the sound of his voice or step, but he knows that *I* have his number. I know that he is a coward, a great sneaking bully. He can lord it over small men and women and half-witted Indian boys. He never employs stronger or bigger men than himself. A giant in stature and a Samson in strength, nevertheless he knows that I know he is a coward, a big unwhipped bully.

So much for Bull Langdon. My paper feels soiled from the printing of his name upon it. He is the worst type of his sex. I am aware, of course, that there are some decent members of the male species. It's true I have not met many. Still there are some. I suppose among the few I might include that Scotch doctor who persists in paying me monthly visits just as if I needed either his advice or his pills. When I say "decent," I do not mean to be especially complimentary. He has many unendurable traits of character. In the first place he is painfully, hopelessly Scotch. Also peculiarly dense and thick. It's impossible to snub or even insult him. I long ago abandoned the attempt to make him understand that I was not keen upon having him call upon me. I flatly stated that I was satisfied with my own company. He merely grunted in reply, and came around the following month as punctually as ever. He is a grouchy, quarrelsome, contentious man, and I believe comes mainly for the pleasure of finding fault and to criticize me and vent his disapproval of me and my mode of life and dress.

However, one cannot quarrel with a man who, in a way, has helped to save one's life. No doubt if he had not cared for me when I first arrived in Alberta, I should be dead now. I am, or was, what they call in the west "a lunger." I was definitely diagnosed as "T.B." and the X-rays have revealed that I possess but one lung; but if anyone doubts that that one lung is sound and strong, he should hear me let out a war whoop, that might compare very well with Chief Pie Belly's. Pie Belly is a Stoney Indian, and I heard him hi-yi-i-i-i-ing one day. Not that I make a daily practice of war-whooping. Still there is sport in owtting the full volume and force of one's lungs (I mean lung in my own case) pour out across the utter stillness of the vast prairie. If my voice carries to my neighbours—the nearest is five miles off—no doubt they take me for a coyote. Nettie Day—the Days are my nearest neighbours, with the exception of the homestead going up on the adjoining quarter—Nettie Day says she has heard me, but then Nettie has a sort of psychic sense. Once she told me she could hear me *think*. Strange words from a poor, illiterate, ignorant young girl.

I confess to a special feeling for Nettie. I am not likely to forget her face as it hovered above my own when first I saw her. Sickness, delirium even may cast a glamour over things. It may be that then we picture things as they are not; but Nettie's face, with its gentle look of tenderness and compassion, seemed to me as sweet and lovely as the "blessed damozel's," as she looked down from the wide arch of heaven to the earth beneath. A dream, no doubt, but I have never been able to efface it.

Next to my place is a quarter section of homestead land, owned by a young man named Stanley. One day I was fencing—when this young fellow, who made several ineffectual attempts to pick an acquaintance with me, came over and watched me at work. I ignored him, but like my doctor friend he is Scotch and thick. He didn't even know he was being ignored, and presently, in a disgustingly cheerful and friendly way, he attempted to tell me how to make postholes. I turned around and looked at him. Now I may look, as I have been called, like a "tough old nut," but I know the English trick of freezing ordinary people by a mere look. It *is* a trick, like the Englishman's monocle, and the strange part is, only an English person can do it. You just stare, stonily, at the despised atom before you. I begin at the feet and travel contemptuously up the whole despised body, till I reach the abashed and propitiating face. One need not say a single word. That look—if you know the technique of the act—is enough. This young Stanley dropped his hammer in a hurry and turned very red.

"'Say, you're not mad at me, are you?" he stammered.

And just then Nettie, whom the doctor had dropped at my house that day, came from out the house, and something about that boy's face, just a flicker of the eye and a deepening red about his ears, apprised me of the reason why he was so keen on being friends with me. I turned just in time to see on Nettie's guilty face the identical flicker I had noted on Stanley's. As cross as two sticks, I grabbed that girl by the arm and shoved her along the field to the house.

Once inside, I made her sit down, while I told her in detail all the miseries and pitfalls, and deceits and heartbreaks, the general unhappiness that befalls one foolish enough to fall in love. Love, I told her, was an antiquated emotion which had been burned out by the force of its own mad fire. I said something like that, for I was talking with feeling upon a topic I understood, but, pausing a moment, I discovered that Nettie's gaze was far away, and I am sure that she had heard not one word of my discourse. She said, simply:

"Thank you, Miss Angel," as humbly and meekly as if I had given her something sweet, and she leaned over, just like a child, and kissed me. The touch of Nettie's soft lips against my cheek, I will confess, was not unpleasant, and I do not know why it had the effect of making me suddenly conscious of an overwhelming desire to put my head down upon the girl's shoulder and weep—I who long ago left far, far behind me that symbol of the weak—tears.

That young man on the adjoining quarter sings as he works. He has a real voice, a clear, fine baritone, and in the still evenings, I confess there is something uplifting about his fresh young voice as it rings across the prairie. His home is nearing completion, he says, and that is why he sings. The thought of home and Nettie warms his heart till it bursts into song. Ah, well, who am I to judge what is best for these young people? So, sing on, young Cyril. I hope that that clear brave voice of yours, as full of melody as a lark's, will never falter.

Last night, when I came in from the field, the half-breed Jake sidled along from behind my house. It gave me a start to see the poor idiot with his wild, witless face. He wanted to tell me something about the Bar Q. He jabbered and jibbered, and I could hardly make head or tail of what he was saying, save that Bull Langdon was eating something up.

CHAPTER X

BRIGHT SUNLIGHT FLOODED ALBERTA. The miraculous harvest was over, and the buzz of the thousand threshing machines, day and night, sounded like music in the ears of the ranchers. The greatest bumper crop in the history of the continent had made Alberta famous throughout the grain world.

Settlers were pouring in from "across the line." Land values soared to preposterous heights; where were miles upon miles of open range and unbroken land, the territory was being staked and fenced.

On the wings of the famous crop came first the fatal oil and then the fatal city real estate boom, which later was to act as a boomerang to the land, since it brought in the wildcat speculator, the get-rich-quick folk, the gold-brick seller and the train of clever swindlers that spring into being when a boom is in swing. The great province was to be exploited by these parasites. The boom swelled to overwhelming proportions almost overnight. The streets of Calgary were thronged—train loads poured into the country; hysterical, half-crazed gamblers and "suckers" made or lost fortunes overnight; businesses of all kinds were started on a "shoe-string;" the wildest stories of oil flowing like water raced about the land. Oil indeed there was, as also coal in unlimited quantities, for the mineral wealth of the province was barely scratched, but the boom raged into being before the tests were properly made, with the result that conservative people began to regard it askance, and almost as quickly as it had grown into being, like an inflated bubble, the oil boom burst. This brought upon the country undeserved desertion and wholesale ruin. Alberta had been made the "goat" of a flock of get-rich-quick men, intent on booming a wealth, which, then, existed only upon paper.

The one solid and substantial asset that all the deflated booms could not affect was the agricultural wealth of the province, real and potential. During this period, Bull Langdon's power and wealth swelled to enormous proportions. Before the year was out, he had become a multi-millionaire. His cattle ranged, indeed, over those "thousand hills;" his hundreds of granaries were bloated with the grain of a bumper crop—grain that he held to sell when the market suited him; his grip was upon the stockyards and packing-house industry, and the livestock market was under his control. There was no one who questioned his right to be called the Cattle King of Canada.

Bloated with affluence and power, illiterate and uncouth, his vanity was immense. It flattered him to be known as the richest and most powerful man in the province; to have his cattle, his stock, his immense ranches pointed out; to see his brand far-flung over the cattle country and encroaching into the western states; his name stamped upon the beef that topped the market, not merely in the west but the east, and reaching out into the Chicago stockyards—there to be exhibited and wondered over—grass-fed steers, competing with and excelling the cornfeds of the U.S.A.

Above all his possessions he placed his magnificent purebred Hereford bulls, a race whose stamp was upon the whole cattle country, for scarcely a farmer or rancher in the country but aspired to have his herd headed by a Bar Q bull. He had spared no expense or labour upon the breeding of these perfect animals, the sires of which had come from the most famous herds in England and the States, and the mothers pure Canadian stock.

He coveted now the world championship for his latest product, a two-year-old Hereford bull, Prince Perfection Bar Q the Fourth. The Prince, as he was known throughout the pure breed world, was of royal ancestry, and already, as a mere calf, his career at the cattle fairs in Canada had brought him under the eyes of the experts and cattle specialists. He was the son of that Princess Perfection Bar Q the Third, who had brought the lordly price, when exhibited in Chicago, of $40,000. His sire was of foreign birth, shipped to Canada by a member of the royal family, who, infatuated with the "cattle game," had acquired a ranch in Canada, and declared it to be the sport of kings.

Annually, there was a showing of the Bar Q bulls, and from far and near ranchers trekked from all over the continent to see the latest products of the famous herd. This year was exceptional, inasmuch as the two-year-old Prince was to be examined and shown before a jury of experts, who would pronounce upon his chances of winning the coveted championship in the United States.

His curly hide brushed, smoothed, oiled and trimmed; his hoofs all but manicured; his face washed with soft oiled cloths; his eyes and nostrils wiped with boracic acid; fed on the choicest of green feed and chop, a golden ring in his nose, through which was a golden chain, the petted brute was led out to gladden the eyes of stock enthusiasts, experts, agriculturists, scientific cattle students, who had come from the four corners of the earth with a passion similar to that of the man of research or the collector, who runs to earth some desired rare article. They crowded about this perfect product of the Hereford race, and looked the massive brute over with the eyes of connoisseurs.

There were in that crowd of men about the roped-in space, around which Cyril Stanley led the bull by the chain, university men, men of title, an English prince, and an ex-president of the United States, millionaire cattlemen and sportsmen. Besides these men, there were the overall cattlemen, ranchers, farmers, stock enthusiasts, stockyard and packing-house men, to say nothing of the humble homesteaders and derelicts, the numerous "remittance men" from the old country, and speculators from other cattle centres. A mixed "bunch," socially as wide apart as the antipodes, but in that cattle shed, as close as brothers. They rubbed elbows, swopped expensive cigars for grimy chews, held their sides at each other's jokes, and joshed and roared across to each other. They were kindred spirits. Cattle represented the bond between them.

Glowering and grinning at each other, as at a prize fight, applauding, groaning out oaths of enthusiasm, strange explosive utterances, they made a motley circle. Professor Martin Calhoun made a telescope of his hands, and squinted through it with screwed up eyes, the attitude of an artist before a masterpiece. After a long scrutiny, he shook his head and moaned with joy.

Through this group of men moved Bull Langdon, in high good humour, dominant and arrogant, intimate with everyone, yet curiously close to no one. When the big shed-tent was full, and the circle about the ropes entirely surrounded his exhibit, Bull Langdon nonchalantly stepped into the ring, where the Prince followed Cyril Stanley tamely about. Cyril had an hypnotic effect upon the animal, who submitted even to having his head caressed and his nose patted.

On either horn two bright ribbons had been coyly twisted and tied, and this slight bedizenment gave him a peculiarly festive look. As Bull Langdon stepped into the ring, a murmur of admiring and respectful applause broke forth. He approached the Prince from the left side, and reaching out a careless hand, pulled the ribbon from one of the horns.

"We ain't raisin' no dolls!" said the cowman. "This is a *Bull!*" and he reached for the other horn.

"Careful, boss!" warned Cyril. "He's not used to all this excitement, and I got my hands full keeping him calm."

"Who's talking?" growled the cattleman, spitting with amusement. "Are you trying to teach Bull Langdon the cattle game, you young whelp? I knowed it before the day you was born."

The young bull's head had suddenly uplifted. He sniffed the air, his neck bristling. Slowly, growing in depth and power, there burst from his throat a mighty roar that shook the tent, and drove the colour from the faces about the ring, as with almost a concerted movement there was a backing from the lines and an exodus from the tent. Bull Langdon, as swiftly as a cat, had backed to the lines and was over them. Cyril was alone in the enclosure with the roaring bull. He was half talking, half singing, nor for a moment did his hand relax its grip upon the chain. Slowly the animal's head turned to his direction and again dropped submissively. There was a breath of relief about the lines, and Cyril led the bull back to his stall. By the ring in his nose, he was securely fastened to a post.

Bull Langdon was swearing foully, but his fury against Cyril and the Prince was abated by the approach of Professor Calhoun, the greatest authority on pure-bred cattle in the world.

"Sir," said the little man, glaring at Bull Langdon through double-lensed glasses—something in his scientific scrutiny of the cattleman not unsimilar to the examination of the cattle themselves—"I will not hesitate to predict that your animal's progress throughout the United States—I will go further and say throughout the world—will be one of unbroken triumph. It has been my pleasure to look upon the most perfect specimen of the Hereford race in the world. I congratulate you, sir."

Bull Langdon grunted, rose on the balls of his feet, chewed on the plug in his cheek, spat, and his chest swelling, roared across to one of the Bar Q hands.

"Take the gentleman—take all of the gentlemen"—he added, with a sweeping gesture of his arm toward the crowd, "to the booze tent. The treat's on Bull Langdon. Fill up, gentlemen, on the Bar Q."

Meanwhile, satiated with gloating over his great treasure, he bethought him of another possession, and upon which at this stage he set, it is possible, an even greater value. True, he reckoned Nettie as "scrub" stock, while the Prince was of lordly lineage. On the auction block, the Prince might bring a price that was worth a king's ransom; yet as he thought of the big white-skinned, blue-eyed girl, the cowman knew that he would not give her up for all the champions in the cattle world. He owned the Prince; he had held the girl in his arms, but in his heart of hearts he knew that she had never been his own. That was what fretted and tormented him—the thought that his brand upon Nettie could never be permanent.

It was a boast of the cowman that what he craved he took. What he took, he held. He had craved Nettie Day. He had taken her by mad foree, as a barbarian might have fallen upon a slave; yet he knew, with a sense of smouldering hatred and fury, that a single hair upon the head of the young Bar Q hand was more to her than the Bull and all his possessions. He was torn by a consuming desire to return to Bar Q and again take forcible possession of her; but the prize herd was now almost ready for the tour. It would be disastrous to his reputation and career if at this psychological moment, anything should interfere with the departure of the herd, and there was no man in the outfit who could be trusted to take the place of Bull Langdon himself. Well, it would be a matter of a month or two only, and he would be back.

He found himself at the stall of the Prince, glowering down upon the back of the kneeling Cyril, brushing down his charge's legs with an oiled brush. Presently Cyril looked up, and seeing his employer he arose. The Bull cleared his throat noisily.

"Well, how about it, bo? You goin' along with the Prince to the States?"

Cyril waited, in his slow way, before replying, and as he hesitated, the Bull threw in savagely:

"Bonus of $500.00 to the hand that takes special charge of the Prince, and another $10.00 raise to his wages."

Five hundred dollars! It was a mighty sum of money, and the young man felt his heart thump at the thought of what it would buy for Nettie.

"When would you want me to leave?"

"Two weeks."

"When'd we be back?"

"Two months. I'll go along as far as St. Louis; leave for a spell, and join you at Chicago, comin' back with the outfit."

"I'd want a week off."

"What for?"

"I got a bit o' fencing to finish on my homestead, and I got to ride over to Bar Q."

Cyril's straight glance met his.

"My girl's there."

"Who'd you mean?"

"Nettie Day. We're planning to get married this winter."

The savage in Bull Langdon was barely held in check. He could scarcely control the impulse to throttle the life out of the cool-eyed youth, who dared to claim for his what was the Bull's.

"You're countin' your chickens before they're hatched, ain't you?" he snarled. "Mebbe the gell's stuck on someone else."

"Not on your life, she's not," said Cyril with calm conviction. "She and me are promised."

"Beat it then," roared the Bull, "and the sooner you're back the sooner we'll start. I'll hold the job for you for two weeks—not a day longer."

"You can count on me," said Cyril. "I'll be on the job."

CHAPTER XI

EVERY DAY NETTIE AROSE AT SIX and went about her dull duties. There was the cream to separate, the pails and separator to clean and scald, there was the butter to make, the chickens to feed, washing, ironing and cleaning. The canning season was at hand, and the Indians rode in with wild cranberries, gooseberries, raspberries and saskatoons. From day to day she picked over and washed the fruit, packed it in syrup jars, and set them in the wash boiler on the stove.

Time accustoms us even to suffering, and one of the penalties of youth and health is that one thrives and lives and pursues his way, even though the heart within him be dead. In a dim sort of way Nettie groped for a solution to her tragedy. She knew that it was not something that could be pushed away into some obscure recess of the mind. It was something unforgettable, a scald upon the soul rather than the body. Of Cyril she could think only with the intensest anguish of mind, and she knew that never could she face the man she loved and tell him what had befallen her. Already he had come to exist in her mind only as one dear and dead. He was no longer for her. She had lost Cyril through this act of Bull Langdon.

Two weeks after the departure of the Bull for the purebred camp, Nettie was startled at her work by the insistent ringing of the telephone, which had been entirely silent since then. Her first thought was that the Bull was calling from Barstairs, and the thought of his hateful voice, even upon the wire, held her back. The telephone repeated its ring, and with lagging feet, Nettie at last answered it.

"Hello!"

"Is that the Bar Q?"

It was a woman's voice, quavering and friendly. Nettie's hand tightened in a vice around the receiver. Her eyes closed. Pale, breathless, she leaned against the wall.

"Is that Bar Q? Is that you, Nettie?"

"Yes, ma'am."

"Is Mr. Langdon home?"

"No, ma'am."

"Any of the men about?"

"They're all in the fields."

"That's too bad. I'm here at the station. Came down on the noon train. 'Twould take too long for you to harness up and meet me, so I'll go over to the Reserve, and maybe Mr. Barrons will bring me up. Good-bye, Nettie. Is everything all right?"

A pause, and then Nettie answered faintly:

"Yes, ma'am."

Nettie hung up the 'phone and stood with her face pressed to the wall. A great tide of fear and shame swept over her. How was she to face her gentle mistress? How speak to her? How find words to tell her? She longed to escape from the kind and questioning eyes that would look so trustingly and fondly into her own.

It was but half an hour's run by automobile from the station, and the grating noise of the car trying to make the high grade to the house brought Nettie violently back to life. She dabbed at her eyes with her apron, smoothed her hair and tried to compose herself as best she could as the little car chugged to the back door.

An appalling change had taken place in Mrs. Langdon. Despite her feeble protest, the Indian Agent in whose car she had come insisted on lifting the frail little woman from the automobile, and he carried her into the house. She tried to laugh, as Nettie placed a chair for her, and when breath would permit it, she cried out bravely:

"Well, here I am, Nettie, back like a bad penny, and feeling just fine!"

Fine! when there was scarcely nothing left of her but skin and bones. Fine! when she was so weak she could scarcely stand without support. Nettie knelt in a passion of mothering pity beside her, and removed the little woman's coat and hat. Meanwhile, the faint tingle of her mistress's chiding laughter hurt Nettie more than if she had struck her.

"Why, Nettie, one would think I was a baby, the way you are fussing over me. I really feel *very* well. I'm in perfect health. We all are, dear, you know. Illness is just an error of the imagination, just as sin and everything that is ugly and cruel in the world is. We are all perfect, made in God's image, and we can be what we will. Why, Nettie, dear, what on earth—!"

Nettie's head had fallen upon her mistress's lap. Unrestrained great sobs shook and tore her.

"Nettie! Nettie! I'm real cross with you. This won't do at all. Don't you see that by giving way like this, we bring upon ourselves illnesses and troubles? We really are manufacturers of our own ills, and the solution of all our problems is right within ourselves."

Nettie raised her head dumbly at that, and sought to choke back the overwhelming sobs.

"Mrs. Langdon, I can't never leave you now."

"Never leave me! Were you thinking of going then?"

"Oh, yes, Mrs. Langdon, I thought I'd *have* to go. There—were reasons why, and—"

"Nettie, if the reasons are Cyril, I know all about it. You can't possibly marry till he gets back. Bill wants him to go to the States with the bulls."

"Mrs. Langdon, I can't never marry Cyril Stanley. I'd die first. Oh, Mrs. Langdon, I wish't I was dead. I wish't I had the nerve to drown myself in the Ghost River."

"Nettie Day, that is downright wicked. Whatever's come over you? Have you fallen out with Cyril? You've been brooding here alone. Now I'm back, things will right themselves. I want you to be the cheerful girl I'm so fond of—so very fond of, Nettie."

Very slowly, but bravely, waving back the help Nettie proffered with outstretched hand, Mrs. Langdon moved to the stairs, smiling and reiterating softly her health formula:

"I am strong, in perfect health, in God's image, His creation. All's well with me and God's good world."

Nettie watched her as slowly she climbed the stairs. There was the sound of the closing door, and then the hollow, wrenching, barking cough. Words of the Bull flashed like lightning to her mind:

"My old woman ain't strong. She'll croak soon. There'll be another Mrs. Langdon at Bar Q. You—"

Nettie's hand went to her strangling throat. Her voice rang out through the room with its tone of wild despair:

"Oh, my God!" prayed Nettie Day. "Don't let Mrs. Langdon die. Don't let her die. Please, please, please. Oh God, let her live!"

CHAPTER XII

THE LONG, GOLDEN FALL OF ALBERTA was especially beautiful that year, and although it was now well into November, the weather was as warm and sunny as the month of May. Winter came late there, sometimes failing to show its frosty hand till considerably after Christmas; but it stayed late, encroaching upon the spring. There was a common saying that there really was no spring in Alberta. One stepped directly from winter into summer. But the fall was incomparably beautiful. The days were laden with sunlight, and the night skies, with their trillion stars, that spotted a heaven more interesting and beautiful than anywhere else on earth, was remarkable for its night rainbows and white splashes of Northern Lights.

Yet the long, sunlighted days, and the cool, star-spotted nights, carried no balm to the distracted Nettie. She felt sick in body and soul.

As she trailed listlessly across the barnyard, she no longer chirruped happily to the wee chicks or reproved the contentious mother hens. The joy of the work and the contact with the live things of the ranch were all gone for her. She was like a machine, automatically wound up. There were certain duties daily to be done. She went about them dully and mechanically.

Basket in hand on an evening late in November, she came from out the cowbarn, where she had been seeking eggs in the stalls, when Jake raced through the yard on his bronco, shouting and screaming with excitement.

"Him! Him!" he yelled wildly, pointing toward where along the Banff highway a solitary horseman could be seen. At the word "Him," Nettie's first thought was of the Bull, and she stiffened and paled; but as she looked down the slope to where the rider was passing through the main gate to the road, she turned even whiter, and a fainting sense of longing and fear shook her, so that she could barely keep from swooning. She well knew that wide hat, that bright flowing scarf, loosely tied beneath the boyish chin, those orange-coloured chaps, the peppery young bronco that was bearing him now so swiftly up the slope. She could not recover from her first emotion at sight of him, to flee, as now was her panic-stricken impulse, for Jake had opened the gate of the corral. Cyril passed through, saw the girl at the barn door, and leaped from his horse. In an instant he was at her side.

The basket of eggs in her hand crashed to the ground. She lifted up both her hands, and her glance went hither and thither like a trapped thing, seeking some place of escape, as steadily, his face aglow, he closed in upon her. With a muffled cry, she beat him back from her, crying loudly:

"No-o! No! No!"

Like one possessed of a sudden madness and strength, she pushed him from her and ran through the corral and out into the yard. Dumbfounded, Cyril looked after her, and then, calling her by name, he pursued her.

"Nettie! Nettie! I say—Nettie!"

She fled like one possessed, running in a circle round the house, then darting in at the back kitchen door. She tried to hold the door closed, but his impetuous hand forced it open. Her breath coming in spasmodic gasps, leaning against the wall of the back kitchen for support, Nettie faced him.

She cried out loudly:

"Go away! Go away!"

"Go away! What do you mean? What for? Nettie, for God's sake! What's the matter, little girl?"

She repeated the words wildly, with all the force in her power.

"Go away! Go! Don't come near me. Don't touch me. Don't even look at me."

"Why not? What's the matter? You're playin' a game, and it ain't fair to go so far. What's the matter, girl? Nettie—you—you ain't gone back on me, have you?"

She could not meet those imploring young eyes, and turned bodily about, so that now her face was to the wall and her back to him. Her voice sounded muffled, strangled.

"Leave me be. I mustn't see you."

"Why not? Since when? What've I done? I got a right to know. What's happened?"

His voice quavered, though he sought manfully to control it. There was a long, tense silence, and then Nettie Day said in a low dead voice:

"I ain't the same."

"You mean you've changed?" he demanded, and she answered in that same dead voice:

"Yes—all changed. I ain't the same."

He took this in slowly, his hands clenching, the hot tears scalding his lids. Then burst out with boyish anguish and passion:

"Don't say that, Nettie. I can't believe it. It ain't true. You and me—we're promised. I been thinking of nothing else. I built the little house for you. It's all ready now, dear, and I come on up to Bar Q now to tell you I got a chance to go to the States with the pure-bred stuff, and there's a bonus of $500.00 in it for me, and a $10.00 raise in my wages. Nettie, girl, I took him up on that proposition because I wanted to do more for you."

"Why did you go away?" said Nettie harshly.

"I went on your account. You ain't mad about that, are you, girl? Why, I wanted to make things softer for you, and I got a chance now to make good money— $500.00, Nettie, and I says to myself: 'Here's where Nettie and me'll go off on our honeymoon to the U.S.,' and I come up here now thinking, 'Here's where we'll put one over on the Bull, and we'll slip down to Calgary and get married, and when we get aboard the train, I'll spring my wife on the outfit and—'"

He choked and gulped, and Nettie moaned aloud, crying:

"I tell you that I ain't the same. I'm changed. You oughtn't to have gone away."

Dark suspicions began to mount, and with their growth, jealous fury caused him to swing her roughly about, so that again she faced him. But she eluded his glance, turning her head from side to side, so that she need not meet his accusing hot young eyes.

"You got another fellow, have you? Have you? You can answer that anyway."

But there was no answer from the girl, and as his grip relaxed on her arms, her head dropped dumbly down. A cruel laugh tore from between the boy's lips.

"I see! Someone's cut me out, heh? I'm dead on to you now. I got your number, I have. If you're that sort—if you couldn't stand a few months' separation without goin' back on a fellow, I'm well rid of you. I wish you luck with your new fellow. I hope he ain't the fool like I been."

Still there was no answer from the girl, standing there with her head dropped, and her arms hanging like a dead person's by her sides.

Presently there was a clatter of hoofs in the corral, and Cyril went out at a furious trot. As over the hills the flying horseman disappeared, Nettie slowly sank to her knees, and, her arms stretched out, she cried aloud:

"I wish't I was dead! I wish't I was dead!"

CHAPTER XIII

CYRIL REACHED THE PURE-BRED CAMP the following morning. He had ridden without stopping all of the previous night. His mind was a hot chaos. He suffered all the torments of jealousy and uncertainty. Even though he told himself that he now hated Nettie, his heart coiled in aching tenderness about her. He pictured her as he had known her—her hair shining in the sun, and that look which love alone brings to human eyes, lighting up her face and making it divinely beautiful to her lover. He thought of Nettie at the little shack, where she had helped him fashion some of the rude pieces of furniture; of a ride across the prairie, their horses' necks touching as the girl and boy pressed as closely to each other as the horses would permit; of Nettie meeting him nightly in the berry bushes; of her hand nestling in his own. Nettie in his arms, her lips upon his!

In the darkness of the night, the boy rode sobbing. In the grey of the morning, red of eyes, his hat well over his face, he pulled into the Bull camp, and with as steady a gait and voice as he could command, he faced Bull Langdon.

"You back already?"

"Yes."

"Ready to go on?"

"Yes."

"Good. We'll get away a few days ahead. Hold on, there!"

Cyril had moved to go. He stood now at the door of the cattle-shed.

"Where've you been?"

There was no answer, and the Bull persisted.

"You been to Bar Q?"

"Yes."

"Well?"

There was silence again, and the Bull cut in with seeming indifference.

"How's your gell? When you gettin' married?"

A deep pause, and Cyril answered slowly:

"It's off. I ain't marryin'."

"Turned you down, did she? Huh! Well, what do you care? There's plenty good fish in the sea. There ain't nothing to bellyache about. When you get over to the States, you'll get all this female guff out of your bones. Women ain't no good anyways. They ain't worth fretting about. They're a bad lot. Gimme *cattle* in preference."

He extended the plug of tobacco, which the boy ignored. His reddened eyes looked levelly into the Bull's, and he said sturdily:

"It's a lie what you said about women. They ain't bad."

CHAPTER XIV

SHUT IN ALL THAT WINTER, which was made up of spells of bitter cold that came on the wings of the blinding blizzards, dissipated by the tempering warmth of Chinook winds, Nettie and Mrs. Langdon were thrown upon their own resources, and drew closer together.

As the winter progressed, something of the girl's strange depression reacted upon the spirits of the sick woman, so that she too lapsed into long spells of silence. She would lie on the couch in the dining-living-room, close to the radiator, propped up high with the pillows Nettie piled around her, her book on Health and Happiness held loosely in her thin hands, as over and over again she repeated the lessons therein taught. Beautiful were those lessons. Surely no one who read could fail to find at least that crumb of hope and comfort that means so much to the hungry heart.

Occasionally her attention would stray from her beloved book, and then she would lie there idly and absently watching the silent Nettie, as she moved about her duties. One day, watching her more intently than usual, and puzzling over the change in the formerly light-hearted and happy girl, something about her movements, a certain lassitude of expression, brought a startling pause to the thought of her mistress. At first she put the idea from her as fantastic and impossible; but moving from her position the better to scrutinize the girl, she was assured that her diagnosis was correct. The book slid from her hand. Mrs. Langdon sat up on her couch, and stared with a startled gaze at Nettie Day. The fall of the book caused the girl to turn from her work, and stooping to pick it up, her glance met that of her mistress.

"Come here, Nettie, I want to speak to you."

Nettie advanced slowly. Some unwilling impulse warned her to hold back, and in her unquiet heart there stirred a dread of the questions she knew were trembling on her mistress's lips. Mrs. Langdon's eyes rose steadily, as she scanned the girl from head to foot.

"Nettie, you are in *trouble!*"

Nettie could not speak for that something that tightened in her throat and held her dry lips pressed.

"Oh, you poor child! You poor little girl! Why didn't you tell me from the first. *Now* I understand!"

Nettie moved around sideways, averting her gaze from those eyes so full of compassion and tenderness.

"Mrs. Langdon," she said, in a low voice, "I ain't done nothing wrong."

"Oh, Nettie, don't deny it, dear. I can see for myself. Sit beside me, dear. I am not condemning you. I only want your confidence. Tell me all about it, Nettie."

"I can't tell you, Mrs. Langdon! I can't. It's something can never be told you."

Nettie was past that stage where tears would have relieved her. All of her senses seemed numbed and hardened, but she clung persistently to the one passionate purpose, to hide the truth at all costs from Mrs. Langdon.

Of all who had known Bull Langdon, his wife alone, despite her cruel experiences with him over the years, did not hate him. To her, he was a child, in error, who, started on the wrong trail, misguided and blind, stumbling in the darkness, had never found his way to that peaceful haven of thought that had been the comfort and retreat of his wife. Incapable of evil herself, she had a child's simple faith in the goodness of others, or their ultimate regeneration from wrong, or error, as she preferred to call it. She never wavered in her faith that sooner or later her "lost lamb" would return to the fold.

Strangely enough, her faith in Bull was probably what had saved her over the years from brutality at his hands. Harsh and gruff and neglectful, he had never been actually cruel to his wife, and he liked defiantly to boast that he had "never raised a hand to her."

Now, as she begged for Nettie's confidence, she had no thought whatsoever of her husband in connection with the girl. That crime. it occurred not to impute to him.

"Do you realize, Nettie, what is about to happen to you?"

"I expect you'll want to turn me out now," said Nettie dully, and then, turning swiftly, she added with sudden force: "But don't do it till the spring, Mrs. Langdon, because you ain't strong enough to do the work this winter, and it's nothing to me, and I want to stay to take care of you."

"Don't you know me better than that? Turn your face around, Nettie. Do you think I'm the kind of woman to turn a girl out because she is going to be what I have all my life longed to be—a mother?"

"Don't! Oh, don't, don't!" cried the girl, loudly, rocking herself in tearless anguish. "I wish't I were dead. I wish't I had the nerve to drown myself in the Ghost River, but now it's all frozen over."

"It's wicked to talk in that way. Why should you wish to drown yourself? I am not judging you. I only want to help you. Cyril—"

"Please don't, Mrs. Langdon."

"Don't what?"

"Don't speak his name, even."

"Why not? Why should you carry this burden alone? If there's any blame, it belongs to him, not you."

"No! No! He never done anything wrong. He's not capable of doing wrong to a girl. Please don't say anything about him. I can't bear it!"

"But we must face this thing fairly. You are in an abnormal condition of mind. It's not an uncommon thing. Some women lose their minds at this time. I appreciate all that you have been suffering, and I pity you from the very bottom of my heart."

Nettie said nothing now, but she wrung her hands and clenched them together like one in physical pain.

"Listen to me, Nettie dear. I want you to know that *I* know what it means to be as you are." Her voice dropped to a wistful whisper. "Eight times, dear—just think of that. You know we pioneered in the early days. We didn't always have a grand place like this, and—and—well, in those days, the distances were so great. We were so far from everything—it was just as if we were at the end of the world, and we didn't have the conveniences, or even the vehicles to carry us to places, and the doctors always came too late, or not at all. I lost all my babies. They just came into the world—to go out again; but I always thought that even the weakest of them had not lived in vain, because, you see, they brought something lovely into my life. It was just as if—as if—an angel's wing had touched me, don't you see? It brought to me a knowledge of love—love eternal and everlasting."

She broke off, with that strange, breathless, smiling pause, as if she sought to force upon her pain the elusive joy that she believed came with her dead children into her life. "So you see, Nettie, I don't hold anything against any woman who bears a child, no matter how or where. It doesn't matter what you or Cyril have done. I have great faith in that boy, and I feel he will make it right."

"Mrs. Langdon," said Nettie, in a suffocating voice, "I ask you to believe that he is not to blame for anything wrong about me."

"I won't then. I'll believe the best of you both. We are going to be very happy, all of us. Just think, you are going to be a mother! It's the sublimest feeling in life. I know it, because all my life I've heard baby voices in my ears and in my heart, Nettie, and my arms have ached and yearned to press a little baby to my breast. My own dear little ones have passed, but, Nettie, I'll hold yours, won't I, dear?"

"Oh, Mrs. Langdon, when you talk like that, I feel just as if something was bursting all up inside me. I don't know what to do."

"Do nothing, dear; but look at God's beautiful world. Lift your eyes to the skies, to the sun, to the hills!"

"There's no sun no more," said Nettie. "The days are all dark and cold now, and the hills are all froze too. They're like me, Mrs. Langdon. I'm all froze up inside."

"Oh, but you'll change now. Look, Nettie, it won't be long before they'll be back—my husband and your Cyril. I had a letter. Where is it now? I put it in my book—no, under my pillow. See, what they write."

The paper fluttered in her hand, and she looked up to smile at Nettie. "It was thoughtful of Bill, wasn't it, to have the letter typed. You know he hates to write letters. Poor fellow hasn't had much of an education. You know, Nettie, he came to the school when I was teaching, to learn. It was pathetic, really it was. But now, he's had some stenographer write to tell me that they'll be home in a couple of weeks. They should have been home two months ago, but they've had a terrible time of it in the States. You see, there's a kind of sickness over there—a plague that's running around. It's all over Europe, and now the States. People, he writes, are afraid to go to public places, and everything is closed up. It's a great disappointment for him, poor fellow. He expected so much from the Prince, and he's hung on from week to week, and been through all sorts of aggravating times. You know they even quarantined his herd on a false suspicion of disease, when they were in *perfect* health. But never mind, we have to have disappointments in life. All I'm thankful for now is that he's coming back—he and Cyril."

Nettie said in a low voice:

"Mrs. Langdon, I don't want to see neither of them again. I can't."

"That's the way you feel now. It's part of your malady. I had notions, too. Wanted the strangest things to eat, and had *such* fits of crying about nothing at all. You'll be all over these moods by the time Cyril rides in. My! I'm going to scold that boy. Yes, yes, you may be angry if you want, but I'm going to give him a real piece of my mind, and then— well, it's never too late to mend a wrong, Nettie."

"Mrs. Langdon," said Nettie violently, "I tell you, Cyril Stanley never did me any wrong."

"Well, that's how you look at it, Nettie, and maybe you're right. I'm the last person to judge you."

Nettie bent down suddenly, and grasping Mrs. Langdon's thin hand, she kissed it. Then, releasing it swiftly, she arose, threw her apron over her face and ran from the room.

CHAPTER XV

IN THE WINTER THE BAR Q OUTFIT IN THE FOOTHILL RANCH was tapered down to eight men. These were all riders. Men who "rode the fences" and kept them in repair; men who "rode the ranch" and made the rounds of the fields, counted and kept account of the cattle remaining on the ranch, and reported to the veterinary surgeon maintained at the ranch when sick or crippled were found.

The breeding stock had been dispatched to the prairie ranch in the fall. Here they were especially housed and cared for. The beef stock, three-year-old steers, were also disposed at the grain ranch, where they were fed on chop and green feed and hay, in process of fattening for the spring market.

The pure-bred heifers and cows had their own home at Barstairs, where also was the camp of the pure-bred bulls.

At the foothill ranch, there was left only the younger stuff, the yearling and rising two-year-old heifers and steers, and these sturdy young stock "rustled"' over the winter range, finding sufficient sustenance to carry them through the winter.

Nettie, long ignorant of her condition, had from day to day passed out the supplies to the men, unconscious of and indifferent to their scrutiny. She failed to realize that what had become apparent to her mistress, had also been revealed to the cunning eyes of the Bar Q "hands."

Bunkhouses in a ranching country are breed-places for the worst kind of gossip and scandal, and men are addicted to this disgusting habit to a worse degree than women. It was, therefore, not long before Nettie's name became first whispered and then carelessly bandied about among them. Eyes were rolled, winks and coarse laughter were the rule in discussing her, who but a little while before had been the object of their admiring respect and desire.

Cyril Stanley's name was also on each man's tongue. That he was responsible for Nettie's condition seemed evident. Following the loose talk and thought of Nettie, came a change in their manner toward the girl. A certain unabashed staring, a familiarity of speech, and presently, worse than that. "Pink-eyed" Tom, a man whose filthy boasts anent women were a source of endless fun among the men, came to the house after a side of bacon. He followed Nettie into the big store-room, where was hung the meat supply of the Bar Q. As she passed the bacon to him, "Pink-Eye" managed to seize her hand, and grinning widely in her face, he squeezed it and attempted to draw her to him. It was only a moment's grasp, but it, and the man's chuckle, sent the girl first deathly white, and then flaming with angry colour.

"Guess you ain't used to man-handling. Oh, no!" said Tom, as she fiercely withdrew from his grasp. He laughed in her face, with an ugly meaning leer that made her heart beat frantically.

She flew from the store-room to the kitchen, and stood with her back pressed against the door, holding it closed. A sickening fear of the whole race of men consumed her. She longed to escape to some place beyond their sight, or ken, where she might hide herself with decency and be allowed at least the boon of suffering unmolested and unseen. She had a passionate longing to escape from the Bar Q—to leave for evermore the hateful place where she had been so cruelly imposed upon, where she had suffered beyond endurance. But the thought of leaving Mrs. Langdon hurt her more than the thought of staying, and her mind strayed off, seeking a solution to her appalling problem. She thought of her friend "Angel" Loring, with her cropped hair and men's clothing, and for the first time she comprehended what might drive a woman to do as the Englishwoman had done.

"A bad report runs a thousand miles a minute," says an Oriental proverb. From bunkhouse to farm and ranch-house raced the tale of the girl's fall. It was a morsel of exciting news to those dull souls shut in by the rigid hand of the winter, and lacking imagination and resource within themselves.

On the first Chinook day, women harnessed teams to democrats and single drivers to buggies and took the road to Bar Q. Never had that ranch been favoured with so many visitors. Neither Nettie nor her mistress suspected that their guests had come to see for themselves, whether there was truth in the story concerning the girl. It had percolated over the telephone, and was brought by riders who hastened along their journey intent upon retailing the latest sensation of the foothills. Caste exists not in a ranching country like Alberta, save among a few rare and exclusive souls, and a hired girl on a ranch had her own social standing in the community, especially if she is that *rara avis*, a pretty woman. So Nettie's fall was of as supreme interest to the ranch and farm wife as if instead of being a servant on a ranch she was the daughter of a prosperous farmer. Hired girls are potential wives for the rest of the ranchmen, and many a farmer's wife had begun her career on a cook car.

Nettie, cutting cake and brewing tea in the kitchen, tray in hand, paused, with a white face, on the other side of the door, as the voices of the women close at hand floated through the swinging doors.

"Looked me right in the face, innocent as a lamb, and she—"

"She's six months gone if a day."

"Seem's as if she might've gone straight, being the oldest in the family. You'd thought she'd want to set an example to her little brothers and sisters."

"Pshaw! She should worry."

"Ain't girls awful to-day!"

"When you told me on the 'phone, I couldn't believe it, and I come along apurpose to make sure for myself."

"Well, now you see, though I'm not used to having my word doubted."

"Why, Mrs. Munson, I hadn't the idea of questioning your word; but I thought you hadn't seen for yourself, and got it third-hand."

"I got it straight—straight from Batt Leeson, and *he* ought to know, after workin' more'n ten years at the Bar Q."

"Personally, I made a point of standing up for the girl."

The voice this time was a shade gentler, but it was also flurried and apologetic.

"You know as well as I do, Mrs. Young, if a girl acts decent, men let her alone. You can't tell me!"

Her face stony, her head held high, Nettie pushed the door open with her foot, and came in with a tray. She silently served them, but her glance flickered toward her mistress, who was leaning forward listening to the whispered words of Mrs. Petersen, cringing toward the rich cattleman's wife. For the first time since she had known her, Mrs. Langdon's voice sounded sharp and cold.

"I'll thank you not to repeat a nasty tale like that. Nettie Day has just as much right to have a child as you have."

"Why, I'm a married woman," blurted the outraged farm wife.

"How do you know Nettie isn't married?"

Chairs were hunched forward. The circle leaned with pricked up ears toward the speaker.

"*Is* she, now?"

"Well, that accounts for it!"

"You couldn't make me believe Nettie was that kind. We all thought—well, you know how girls carry on to-day, I'm sure you'll excuse me. We're all liable to make mistakes."

To Nettie the Inquisition had turned directly.

"My word, Nettie Day, why didn't you let us know? What on earth did you want to keep it secret for? The whole country'd turned out to 'Chivaree' for you. We haven't had a marriage in a year, and Cyril Stanley is mighty popular with the boys."

Nettie's gaze went slowly around that circle of faces. She wanted to make sure that all might hear her words.

"I ain't married to Cyril Stanley, and he done me no wrong. You got no right to talk his name loose like that."

An exclamatory silence reigned in her room. Mrs. Langdon, her cheeks very flushed, was sitting up, her bright eyes, like a bird's, scanning the faces of her visitors.

"Nettie," her thin, piercing voice was raised, "you forgot my tea, and—and—maybe you ladies'll excuse me to-day. I'm not well, you know."

For the first time since she had become a convert to her strange philosophy, she was admitting illness; but she was doing it in another's behalf.

As the last of the women disappeared through the door, and before the murmur of their voices outside had died out, Mrs. Langdon made a motion of her hands toward Nettie, and the girl ran over, dropped on her knees by the couch, and hid her face in her mistress' lap.

"Nettie, don't you mind what they say. Women are terribly cruel to each other. I don't know why they should be, I'm sure, for I believe that we all have in us the same capacities for sinning, only most of us escape temptation. It's almost a gamble, isn't it, Nettie, and I'm so sorry, poor child, that you should have been the one to lose." Her voice dropped to a whisper. "I'll confess something to you now, Nettie. *I*—yes, I—almost—"

"If you're goin' to say something about yourself," said Nettie hoarsely, "I don't want to hear it. You ain't capable ever of doing anything wrong."

On the road, the carriages were grouped together. Their occupants leaned out and called back and forth to each other:

"What do you know about that?"

"I'm certainly surprised at Mrs. Langdon. I didn't think she'd hold to anything like that."

"I did, and I'm not a bit surprised. I could 'a told you a thing or two. Birds of a feather flock together, and she—"

Voices were lowered as another woman's reputation was pulled to shreds.

"Well, Mrs. Munson, you don't say so."

"I remember when the Bull first married her. Sa-ay, there was all kinds of talk. Ask anyone who was here in them times."

Murmurs and exclamations, and a woman's voice rumbling out a tale that should never have been told.

"Would you've believed it! And she so sweet and sly of tongue."

"Still waters run deep. You can't trust them quiet kind. I had it direct from Jem Bowers. You know Jem? He was right along when it happened. They were shut in that school house for two whole days, and the door locked and bolted. The Bull himself asked Jem to go for the missionary, and everyone knew Jem was one of the witnesses to the Langdon wedding. Said she looked like a little scared bird, and her eyes were all screwed up with crying, so I guess doing wrong didn't bring *her* no happiness."

"Well, I'd never have believed it if you hadn't told me. I'm going to hustle right off now. I want to stop and see Mrs. Durkin on my way. She couldn't get off to come as they've had the mumps up to their home, and I promised to let her know, and I'll bet her tongue's hangin' out waitin'."

"Well, don't say I said it."

"I won't. I'll say I got it from—from—I'll not name the party. Get up, Kate! My, that mare's smart."

"I like geldings for driving. They aren't so quick, but they're dependable and strong. Good-bye. Will you be at the box social?"

"Sure, what's it for?"

"Oh, them sick folks to the east. Did you hear about that plague sickness they got in the States and sneaked across to Canada, and everybody's scared nearly to death? They've got it awful now in Toronto and Montreal."

"Didn't know it was as bad as that."

"It's something awful out east, I heard. My husband brought home a paper from Calgary and they had the whole front page in headlines about it. Them Yankees brought it in with them when they run away to escape from it in their own country. Wish they'd stay home and look after their own sicknesses 'stead of coming across the line and carrying it along with them. Others have been flying out west here, and they say if we don't look out, first thing we know, Calgary'll have it, and then—well, it'll be our turn. I heard they were shipping all the sick ones out of the city to the country."

The women looked at each other waveringly, licking their lips and whitening with apprehensive fright. They drew their rugs closer about them and said they had to be off as it was getting dark and they didn't want to catch cold as no one ever knew when a change might blow up in the weather, and clouds off to the north looked mighty threatening. In the sudden rush of apprehension, Nettie was for the time forgotten. The clatter and rattle of their wheels was heard along the road, as with whip and tongue they urged their horses homeward.

CHAPTER XVI

ALL NIGHT LONG THE WIND BLEW WILDLY. It raved like a live, mad thing, tearing across the country with tornado-like force.

The house shook and rocked upon its foundations, the rattling windows and clattering doors seeming to be bursting to open.

To the girl, lying wide-eyed throughout the night, almost it seemed as if the wild wind had in its voice the triumphant, mocking tone of the man she loathed. It seemed to typify his immense strength, his power and madness. It was gloating, triumphing, buffeting and trampling upon her.

Nettie was not one given to self-analysis, but, despite her simplicity of nature, she possessed a capacity for immense feeling. Behind her slow thought, there slumbered an overpowering ability to suffer. Now even the elements played their part upon her morbid imagination. She could not sleep for the raging of the terrific wind, the incessant shaking of windows and doors, and all the sounds of a loosely-built old house, rattling and trembling under the ruthless hand of the wind. As she lay in bed, her face crushed in her pillow, her hands over her ears, as though she might crush down the roar of the wind, she could not efface from her consciousness the thought of the man she hated. She was doomed that night to re-live those horrible hours with him again, and when the vision imposed too piercingly upon her fevered mind, she sprang up in bed, and, rocking herself like one half-demented, sat in judgment upon her own acts.

Why had she not killed? Why did she live? Why was she crouched here now upon her bed, when the Ghost River was at hand? True, it was frozen over, but there were great water holes where the cattle came to drink, and into one of these she might throw herself as into a deep well. Oblivion would then come. Her sick mind would not conjure up the loathsome vision of Bull Langdon, and her ears would be deaf to the taunting, beating challenge of the wind, calling to her with an alarming voice, to come forth and fight hand in hand with the fates that had crushed her.

"I got to go out!" she moaned. "I got to go out! I can't live no longer."

She put her foot over the side of the bed, and with her head uplifted in that fatalistic, straining way, she listened to what she fancied in her disordered mind was a voice out of the river, calling to her above the roar of the wind. And as she sat in the dark room, above the raving of the storm, she heard, indeed, a call—a living voice. Instantly she drew up tensely, holding her breath to catch the clearer that faint cry.

"Nettie! Nettie!"

It was her mistress. She was out of bed, fumbling about for the matches.

The Bar Q was fitted with an electric system, but the wires were not connected with the hired girl's room. It was a pitch dark night. Afraid as she had been of the darkness and the elements, the cry of her well-loved mistress awoke all the defensive bravery in her nature, and she called aloud in reply, feeling along the walls, groping her way to the door.

"I'm coming, Mrs. Langdon! I'm coming! I'm coming!"

In the hall she found the electric button, and hurried across to Mrs. Langdon's room. High up on her pillow, breathing with the difficulty of one afflicted with asthma, was the wife of the cattleman. The window was wide open and the shades flapped angrily and tore at the rollers. The face on the bed smiled up wanly at Nettie in the reflected light from the hall.

"Oh, Mrs. Langdon, did you call me? Do you want something?"

"Yes, dear. I thought, maybe, you wouldn't mind closing my window for me. I tried to get up myself, but I had a sort of presentiment that—that—you were awake, and that perhaps you would—would like to come to me."

"Oh, I was awake, wide, wide awake. I couldn't sleep to save myself. Isn't the wind terrible?"

"It's dying down, I think."

"Oh, it's fiercer than ever," cried the girl wildly. "It's just terrible. I can't bear to hear it. I been awake all night. Just seems as if that wind was shoutin' and screamin' and makin' mock of me, Mrs. Langdon. It's banging upon my soul. I *hate* the wind. I think it's alive—an awful thing. It fights and laughs at me. It's driving me mad!"

"Ah, Nettie, you are not yourself these days. It is not the wind, but what is in your heart that speaks. We can even control the wind if we wish. Christ did, and the Christ spirit is in all of us, if we only knew how to use it."

Nettie had closed the window. On her knees by Mrs. Langdon's bed, she was pulling up the covers and tucking them closely about her, and chafing the thin, cold hands.

"You're cold. Your hands are just like ice. I'm going downstairs and heat some water and fill the hot water bag for you."

"No, no, Nettie. You go right back to bed. I'll go down myself by and by, if I feel the need of the bag."

But though Nettie promised to go back to bed, she hurried down to the lower floor. She had no longer any sense of fear of the wind or the darkness. Her mind was intent upon securing the hot water bag, and she built up a fire in the dead range and set the kettle upon it. She was bending over the wood box, picking out a likely log, when something stirred behind her. Still stooping, she remained still and tense. Slowly the Bull's great arms reached down from behind and enfolded her.

The noise of the wind had deadened his approach to the house. He had come through the living room to the opened kitchen door, where the girl was bending over the stove.

She twisted about in his arms, only to bring her face directly against his own. She was held in a vice in the arms of the huge cattleman. His hoarse whispers were muttered against her mouth, her cheek, her neck.

He chuckled and gloated as she fought for her freedom, dumbly, for her thoughts flew up to the woman upstairs. Above all things, Mrs. Langdon must be spared a knowledge of that which was happening to Nettie.

"Ain't no use to struggle! Ain't no use to cry!" he chortled. "I got you tight, and there ain't no one to hear me. I been thinkin' of you day and night, girl, for months now, and I been countin' off the minutes for this."

She cried in a strangled voice:

"She's upstairs! She'll hear you! Oh, she's coming down! Oh, don't you hear her? Oh, for the love of God, let me go!"

The man heard nothing but his clamouring desires.

"Gimme your lips!" said the Bull huskily.

The clip clop of those loose slippers clattering on the stairs broke upon the hush that had fallen in the kitchen. Through all her agony, Nettie heard the sound of those precious little feet, and she knew—she felt—just when they had stopped at the lower step, as Mrs. Langdon clung to the banister. Slowly the wife of the cowman sank to the lowest step. She did not lose consciousness, but an icy stiffness crept over her face; her jaw dropped, and a glaze came before her staring eyes, like a veil.

Putting forth a superhuman effort, Nettie had obtained her release. She sprang passionately to the feet of Mrs. Langdon, and grovelled before her on her knees.

"Oh, Mrs. Langdon, it 'twant my fault. I didn't mean to do no harm. Oh, Mrs. Langdon, I wish't I'd heeded the wind! It must've been warning me. I wish't I'd gone to the Ghost River when it called to me to come."

Mrs. Langdon's head had simply dropped forward, just as if the neck had broken. Nettie, beneath her, sought the glance of her eyes, and saw the effort of the moving lips.

"God's—will," said the woman slowly. "A demonstration—of—God. I had—to leave, Nettie. God's will you—take—my—place."

Across the half-paralysed face something strangely like a faint smile flickered. Then she seemed to crumble up. She lay inert and still against the stairs.

A loud cry broke from the frantic Nettie.

"We've killed her! We've killed Mrs. Langdon!"

"Killed her—nothin'," said the man hoarsely, his face twitching and his hands shaking. "I told you she was 'bout ready to croak, and you heard what she said. You were to take her place. That means—"

Nettie had arisen, and her eyes wide with loathing, she stared at him in a sort of mad fury. Somehow she seemed to grow strong and tall, and there was that which shone like murder in her eyes.

"I'd sooner drown myself in the Ghost River," she said.

Like one gone blind, she felt her way to her room, and this time the man did not follow her.

The wind raved on; the windows shook and doors and casements creaked as if an angry hand were upon them; the white curtains flapped in and out. There was the heavy tramp of men's feet upon the stair; the rough murmur of men's voices in the hall. She knew they were carrying to her room the woman who had died.

Hours of silence intervened. The Bull had gone with his men to the bunkhouse. She was alone in the house with the dead woman. For the first time, a sense of peace, an uplifting pang of exultation swept over the tortured girl, Mrs. Langdon would know the truth at last! There would be no blame in her heart for Nettie—Nettie, who had a psychic sense of the warm nearness and understanding of the woman who had passed.

As she dressed in the darkness of the room, Nettie talked to her she believed was with her, catching her breath in trembling little sobs and laugh of assurance.

"You understand now, don't you, and you don't hold it against me. I didn't mean no wrong—I done the best I could. You don't ask me to stay now that you know, do you, dear?"

The plaid woollen shawl, a Christmas gift from Mrs. Langdon, covered her completely. The gray light of dawn was filtering through the house; the wind had died down. In its place was falling the snow upon the land, soft and pure and crystal. Nettie's face was white as the snow as she came from her room. Mrs. Langdon's door was closed, and hesitating only a moment, Nettie stole to it on tiptoe. With her face pressed against it, she called to the woman inside:

"Good-bye, Mrs. Langdon. Nobody will ever be so good to me in this world as you have been."

She listened, almost as if she heard that faint, sweet voice in reply. Then, perfectly comforted, she wrapped her cape closer about her, and in her rubbered feet, Nettie Day stole down the stairs and out into the storm.

CHAPTER XVII

LONG SINCE THE VETERAN GELDINGS that had pulled Dr. McDermott for years over the roads of Alberta, had been replaced by a gallant little Ford, that purred and grunted its way along the roads and trails in all kinds of weather, and performed miraculous feats over the roughest of trails, across fields, ploughed land, and chugged along sturdily through to the medical man's goal.

Many of the farmers belonged to that type to whom the proverb, "Where ignorance is bliss 'tis folly to be wise," might well be applied. These laughed or pooh-poohed the doctor's warning admonitions in regard to the plague, already as far west as Winnipeg. These "joshed" and "guyed" the man of medicine and asked: "Lookin' for trade, doc? You can't make me sick with your pills, so you better keep them to home. Haw, haw!" And they threw the disinfectant and pills (to be taken should certain symptoms develop) out of sight and mind, and made jokes when he was gone about "Doc's gettin' cold feet like the city guys. If he don't look out he'll be gettin' just like them paper collar dudes in towns and want soothin' syrup for white liver." They hugged to themselves the fatuous delusion that they lived a cleaner and healthier life than mere city dwellers, and hence would prove immune to the diseases that were a peculiarity of the city.

It may not be inappropriate to reflect here upon the fact that country and city hospitals numbered among their patients far more people from the country than the cities, and the Insane Asylums were almost wholly recruited from the farm and ranch houses, where the monotonous pressure of the long life of loneliness took its due toll from those condemned to maddening solitude.

Howbeit, the "doc" kept his stubborn vigil. He did not propose to be caught napping, and he travelled the roads of Alberta, going from ranch to ranch, with his warnings and instructions and despised pills.

While returning from some such expedition into the foothills, he stopped, in the dawn of the day, to fasten the curtains about his car, as the wind of the wild night before had turned with the morning into a snowstorm. A straight, level road was before him, and the doctor counted on making Cochrane in half an hour. Up to this time, despite the weather and the perilous trail to Banff, he had had no trouble with the engine. Now, however, as he cranked, the Ford, a peculiarly temperamental and uncertain car, refused to deliver the spark. He lifted the hood, made an inspection, cranked again and again, held his side and groaned and grunted with the labour of cranking, raged and cussed a bit, regretted the old veterans; then, throwing his dogskin coat over the engine, he sought the trouble beneath. He was lying on his back, a sheepskin under him, tinkering away with the "damned cantankerous works," when, putting out his head to look for the wrench, he saw something approaching on the road that caused him to sit bolt upright with wonder and dismay.

Her cape flapping about her, head freighted with the falling snow, her eyes wide and blank, snow-blind, Nettie Day swept before the wind on the Banff trail. The doctor, on his feet now, blocked her further passage, for she seemed — not to see him, but to be in a trance, as one who walks in sleep.

"What are you doing on the road at this hour, lassie?"

She did not answer, just stared out blankly before her, shaking her snow-crowned head.

A quick professional survey of the girl and the doctor was apprised of her condition and the critical need for early attention. She made no demur; indeed, was touchingly meek, as he assisted her into the car. He tucked the fur robe about her, buttoned the curtains tightly, and, his face puckered with concern, poured a stiff "peg" of whisky. She mechanically drank, gulping slightly as the spirits scorched her throat. Her eyes were drooping drowsily, and when the doctor put his sheepskin under her head, she sighed with intense weariness, and then lay still at the bottom of the car.

The doctor "doggoned" his engine, shoved the crank in, and, miraculously, there was the healthy response of a chug-chug, and the little car roared.

"You're a damned good lad!" gloated Dr. McDermott. He pulled on his dogskin gloves, wiped the frost from the glass, threw a glance back to make sure the girl was all right, and put on top speed.

CHAPTER XVIII

THE LADY ANGELA LORING AROSE AT FIVE IN THE MORNING, put on overalls, sheepskin coat, woollen gauntlets, and heavy overshoes. She tramped through the steadily falling snow to her barn, where were housed a cow, a sow, a mare heavy in foal, a saddle horse and the poultry.

The March winds that had roared all of the previous night had turned with the morning to a snowstorm, and the flakes were now falling so heavily that it was barely possible to see from the house to the barn. Through the blinding flakes the woman rancher plodded to the outhouse.

First she threw the pails of swill and mush prepared and brought from the house into the pig pen. Then she watered the stock, no easy matter, for the pumped water froze in the trough quickly, and she was forced to refill it several times. She climbed then to the hay loft, and with a pitchfork, thrust down through the openings the morning feed for the cow. She carefully measured chop from the bin for the mare, allowing half a pail of oats and a bunch of hay for the saddle horse. She threw to the chickens and hens that had followed hungrily in her wake, a pan full of ground barley and wheat seasoned with cayenne pepper, epsom salts and bits of bones and eggshells.

Finally she fell to milking. The cow was fresh, and she had a full pail. Half of this, however, she fed to the restless little calf, nosing near to its mother, and trying to shake off the muzzle that Angela had snapped on the night before, to prevent the calf from suckling its mother. The task of feeding the calf required patience and time, for the impetuous little "dogie" nearly knocked over the pail, and had to be taught through the medium of the woman's fingers stuck into the pail and thrust, wet with the milk, into the mouth.

She was more than an hour about her chores. With the half-filled milk pail in one hand, she tramped back through the now even more heavily falling snow to the house.

Prior to leaving the house, Angela had lit her fire, and now the place was warm and snug, and the singing kettle gave it an air of cheer. There was that about this poor shack on the prairie, despite its rough bare log walls, and two wee windows, which was not wholly unattractive. Though she chose to wear men's clothing, and had cut her hair like a man's, yet one had only to look about the room to perceive that the eternal feminine had persisted despite her wrathful and pitiful attempt to quench it.

The furniture she had made for the most part herself. They were crude pieces fashioned from willow fence posts and grocery boxes, yet there was evidence of the talent of a craftsman, for the chairs, though meant for utility, were rustic and pretty, and she had touched them in spots with bright red paint. The table, over which a vivid red oil cloth was nailed, was a bright patch of colour in the room. Red, in most places, for decorative purposes, can be used only sparingly, but in a bleak log shack, a splash of its ruddy vigour lends a warmth and cheer that no other colour seems to accomplish. The floor had been scrubbed till it was almost white, and a big red-brown cowhide was thrown near a couch, on which was another hide—a calf-skin. Indian ornaments and bead- work, bits of crockery and pewter, were on the shelves that ranged one side of the shack, where also she kept her immaculately shining kettles, cooking utensils and dishes. A curtain of burlap sacks, edged with some scarlet cloth, hung before the doorway into the bedroom. Here was a bed, scrupulously clean, whose bleached pillow-cases were of flour bags. A large grocer's box, in which shelves had been nailed, was also covered with similar cloth, and served apparently as a sort of dressing table. Two chairs, made from smaller boxes, were padded likewise with the burlap, and a triangular shelf, with a curtain before it, made a closet in the corner of the room.

A huge grey cat followed the woman about the room, sleepily rubbing itself against her, and purring with contentment when she picked it up in her arms.

Angela made her breakfast of oatmeal and tea, serving from the stove directly to her plate. Her cat nestled in her lap while she breakfasted, and she smoothed its coat lovingly.

Time, instead of adding to, had diminished the lines on the face of the woman, and the strained look of suffering in her eyes had been replaced by a clear look of health. Her skin had almost the fresh colour of a girl's. Her hair had grown abundantly, though it still was short and grey in colour; but it curled naturally, and this lent a softening and youthful effect to her face. The spare, lean look of mingled anguish and illness was gone. There was no sign of that appalling disease which had once threatened her life. She looked normal and wholesome as she sat at her table, her cat in her lap, in a brown study. Of what Angela thought when shut in thus alone in her shack it would be hard to say. Long since she had ceased to conjure up bitter visions of the man who was responsible for her father's death and her own exile. Her thoughts, at least, were no longer unbearably painful as in those early days when first she had come to Alberta, and many a day and night, shut in alone with her black secret, Angela had wrestled in bitter anguish with the crowding thoughts that came like ghosts to haunt her.

However, even in the winter, she had little enough time for mere thoughts. Her life was crowded with work. When she had finished her meal, and after having washed her dishes, made her bed, kneaded the dough for her weekly baking, and put a pot of beans, soaked overnight, into the oven, she prepared to go out again. This time, to the pasture, where her few head of stock "rustled" for their feed all winter. A snowstorm at this time of the year is always dangerous for the breeding stock, dropping their calves with the approach of spring. There were, moreover, water-holes in the slough that, frozen over, needed daily to be smashed, so that the cattle might have the much needed water. Angela, axe in hand, opened the door of her shack. A gale of wind and snow almost blinded her, so that at first she did not see the Ford that was ploughing its way noisily and pluckily down the road allowance that led to her house. The honk of the doctor's horn, which he worked steadily to attract her, caused her to peer through the storm, and she turned to the gate where the car had stopped.

She never encouraged the gratuitous visits from Dr. Mc-Dermott, who had saved her life when first she had come to Alberta; but at least she showed no incivility. Time had accustomed her to these regular calls from the country doctor, and, in truth, though she would not have admitted it for anything in the world, she had come to look forward to his visits, and to depend upon them for her news of the world, of which she had so bitterly told herself she was through forever.

Now, his ruddy face was thrust from the curtains, and, frowning slightly, Angela tramped to the car.

"Are you strong enough to lend me a hand lifting something?" demanded the doctor.

"Certainly, I'm strong enough, but what do you mean?"

Dr. McDermott, out of the car now, unbuttoned the back curtains, and revealed to the amazed Angela the still heavily sleeping Nettie.

"There's a sick lass here," he said solemnly, "and a lass in sore trouble, I'm thinking."

A strange expression had come into the face of Angela Loring. Not so long since, it seemed to her, this girl who lay on the floor of the doctor's car, had leaned above her as in a dream and had regarded her with the tender, com-passionate gaze of her own mother. In the days of semi-consciousness that had followed, the Englishwoman could endure the sight and touch of no one but Nettie. She comprehended not what had befallen her friend of those first days in Alberta. All she knew was that Nettie was now as helpless as she had been when the girl had cared for her. Without a word or question, she assisted the doctor to lift Nettie from the car, and to carry her into the house.

CHAPTER XIX

ANGELA LORING BELIEVED that there was nothing about her of which the Scotch doctor approved. He came, she thought, merely to exercise what she called his abnormal habit of fault-finding. Her cut hair he denounced unsparingly. No lass, he declared angrily, had a right to cut the hair from her head that her Maker had planted there. Her man's clothes were unqualifiedly disgraceful. Her work in the field was against Nature. She should chasten her bitter tongue and heart. She should cultivate her neighbours, and she should not set herself up against her fellow men. Her obsession, which is what he termed her aversion to his own sex, and her unnatural life alone was a pathological matter as unfortunate as the disease she had contracted in London, and of which he had cured her. He purposed now to cure her also of what he termed her mental malady.

Angela had let him run along, disdaining to reply, and she pursued her way undeterred by his wholesale condemnation of her course of life.

But now they were working together shoulder to shoulder. It was team work, this long struggle and vigil by the bedside of Nettie Day.

When Angela held in her arms for the first time in her life a little baby, and looked with dewy eyes down upon the small blonde head resting so helplessly against her breast, could she have seen the face of the country doctor, she would have known that all of his thoughts of her were not wholly harsh.

Glaring up at him to mask the strange moisture before her eyes, that threatened to overrun, she could not see that look of grave tenderness that softened the rough face of the man who had known her as a child.

"Look here," said Angela, trying to control a voice that was tremulous in spite of her, "Nettie won't touch it—says she doesn't want it—and worse. Well, I'll take it then. I'll care for it. Is there any reason why I shouldn't have it?" she demanded with something of the jealous fierceness of a mother herself.

"None whatsoever," said the doctor in a voice that was husky. He had a habit when unduly moved of lapsing into Gaelic, and what he muttered now was unintelligible to the woman, absorbed in the baby in her arms. Translated she would have known that the doctor's opinion was that a woman who could mother another woman's bairn, would be a good mother to her own.

Outside the snow was still heavily falling. Great mounds were piling up on all sides. That world of snow might have appalled the stranger, but to the farmer it meant assured moisture in the soil. A spring snowstorm was even more desirable for the land than rain, as it melted gradually into the earth. Already the sun was gleaming through the falling snowflakes, and the intense cold had abated.

"Weel, weel, I'll be off for a while, lass. There's much still to attend to."

"You can't go out in that storm," said Angela roughly. "Wait, I'll get you something to eat. Not even your Ford could plough through snow like that."

"Maybe not, and I'll not be taking the Ford."

"Well, I've no vehicle to lend you."

"I'll go afoot," said the doctor, wrapping his woollen scarf about his neck, preparatory to going out.

"You're a fool to go out," said Angela crossly. "Wait till you have a cup of coffee anyway."

"I'll be going just across the land, to the lad's cabin. I heard last night that he was back."

"Who's cabin? What land?

"Young Cyril Stanley's—the scallawag. I'll have that to say to him, I'm thinking, will bring him across in a hurry."

"He needn't come here!" Angela had started up savagely. "I don't want any man here, least of all a dog like that who'd do such a thing to a girl. He can keep away from *my* house. He's not fit to—to even look at her now. No man is."

"Weel, weel, 'tis true, but we're all liable to mistakes, ma'am, and young blood is hot and careless; and who are we—you and I—to judge another? We must look to our own conscience first, ma'am."

"Yes, stand up for him—defend him. You men all hang together. I know you all, and I hate you. I—"

She broke off, for the doctor was looking at her with such a strange look of mingled power and tenderness that the stormy words died on her lips, and she dropped her wet face upon the soft little one in her arms.

Dr. McDermott closed the door quietly.

CHAPTER XX

THE TOUR OF THE BAR Q pure-bred bulls had been a disastrous and costly one. From city to city, at a staggering expense, went the prize herd, from which extraordinary things had been expected. Wherever they touched, it was their misfortune to be turned back or shunted further afield. That winter, the country was suffering from the fearful scourge, which, having stricken down its victims by the thousands in Europe, had moved over to America.

Followed a time when the Bar Q herd came under the condemnation of an harassed and irritated authority, who under the diagnosis of an incompetent veterinary surgeon, had pronounced the cattle to be suffering from the foot and mouth disease. An order issued for the slaughter of the entire herd, and the burning of all sheds, cars or other houses in which they had been penned. Bull Langdon found himself held indefinitely in the States, as he fought by injunction proceedings the destruction of his herd, which destruction would have meant an incalculable loss to the cattleman— a loss, in fact, that might ruin him.

The adjournments and delays, the long-drawn out legal processes, kept the herd in the States from November to February, and when at last they were freed, the penned-in stuff were in a deteriorated condition. Their long confinement, the unaccustomed travelling and the lack of proper care, made the once smooth bulls cranky and dangerous, so that by the time the herd started back for Canada, more than one of the "hands" who had come to the States with the herd deserted the outfit rather than care for the uncertain animals on tour.

Bull Langdon, raging and fretting over the enforced delays in the States, harassed by his losses and the failure to obtain a showing of the famous herd, was in a black mood when at last the outfit reached Barstairs.

Here a new harassment awaited him. Of all the bulls, the Prince had proven the most dangerous and erratic of temper; his ceaseless bellowing and attempts to obtain his freedom had done much to add to the unpopularity of the outfit upon their travels. Always uncertain and dangerous, back at Barstairs, he became well-nigh uncontrollable, and there was no hand of the entire outfit, save Cyril, who dared approach the raging beast, and behind heavily barred fences he ranged up and down restlessly. Calling and moaning his immense cries to the cattle he could smell even if he could not see in adjoining pastures, something of the wild spirit of the animal appealed to its owner. That savagely roaring bull voiced somewhat of his own pent-up rage. There was a kindred spirit between them. Often, when the exasperations of the tour had fairly choked him with rage, he would go to where the Prince, penned in the limited space of his shed, ranged up and down, bellowing and groaning his outrageous demands for freedom. At such times, Bull Langdon, outside the bars, would call to his animal, not soothingly, but with something of encouragement, a sort of cheering and "rooting" for the fighting brute.

"Go to it," he would snarl through the bars. "Let em know you're here! Keep 'em awake. Make their nerves jump. Go to it, bull!"

Up to the time of the return to Barstairs, Cyril Stanley had cared for the animal, and so long as he was near, the Prince was kept pretty well under control. But Cyril, silent and morose during all the period of their sojourn in the States, now back in Canada, had suddenly decided to quit the outfit. His quiet request to be relieved of his job was heard with consternation and fury by the cattleman.

"What did he want to leave for? Hadn't he had his pay raised four times already? Hadn't he got the promised $500.00?

The herd was practically under his charge, and the foreman's job and wages was in sight before the spring."

Bluster and curses availed nothing, and the mounting sums of money, the heavy bonuses and large salary proffered, were as firmly refused. Money meant nothing now to Cyril. He was heartily sick of the whole business. He had the restless feeling of the man, who, touching home soil again, with all former claims gone, feels the need of moving along the trail. Since home was not for him, and since even absence had not cured him of the malady that the world names Love, he wanted to be about from place to place. He had had enough of cattle. He was done with ranching. To the Bull's inquiry as to what he purposed doing, after a thoughtful pause, Cyril replied directly:

"Think I'll hike for Bow Claire. Plenty of work there, I guess. The river'll be high when the snow begins to melt, and they'll be wantin 'hands' and loggers at the camp."

Meanwhile, Bull Langdon found his hands full at the camp. These were the restless days of labour; when in the employment offices there were a dozen employers for every employee; when wages were mounting; when men looked the boss squarely in the face and made their own terms. The cattlemen had returned at a time when labour was so scarce and independent in Alberta, that many of the farmers were forced to do their own work, or grubbed together with other farmers on shares. It is certain that there was no ranchman in the country who would work with Bull Langdon. Even those whom he had been able in the past to tyrannize over and drive at will, gave him a wide berth. Never had the Bar Q been so short-handed, and the departure of Cyril, who was invaluable among the pure-breds, was a disaster to the Bull camp.

The cowman had been beset with an almost insensate craving for Nettie Day. While in the States she had never been wholly absent from his mind, the distraction and obstacles had kept him so concerned that he had been able to govern the desire for the girl. Back in Canada, his mind reverted incessantly to her.

Watching Cyril Stanley disappear at a slow lope over the hills, it occurred to him that he might be making for Bar Q and Nettie Day. The idea gave him pause. The thought of Cyril and Nettie together was something intolerable and not to be borne. The blood rushed madly to his head, and he saw things redly.

Batt Leeson, a hand who had served directly under Cyril, was, next to him, the best man upon the place. He could be trusted to care for the cattle, was a conscientious workman, but Batt had never been tried with authority. When Cyril's place was offered to him, he became apprehensive and uncertain. However, there was no man at the time at the Bull camp, which had been stripped for the trip to the States, of foreman size.

The Bull chewed over the possibility of Cyril changing his mind and returning to Bar Q. He knew what logging in the lumber camps meant. The work would not daunt the young man, but the food and the dirt would. The daily association with "them damn dirty foreigners," as Bull named the Russian loggers, would soon be too much for a white man. He counted upon Cyril's return.

When he left the camp, he was by no means easy in his mind in regard to his cattle. He took the trail for Bar Q, in his big car, touring along the road in the face of an almost volcanic wind, that yet could not force the big car to deviate from its course. It was late at night when Bull Langdon reached the ranch in the foothills, and the roaring of the wind deadened all other sound, so that when he saw that light in the kitchen, he came warily upon the place, sniffing the air like a bloodhound who tracks to his lair some wounded fugitive. In the dark living room he had watched the motions of the girl at the range with distended eyes.

The blood mounted to his head. All thought was blotted out save the mad desire to crush in his arms the girl for whom he cherished this overwhelming passion.

Meanwhile, Cyril Stanley mechanically had turned his horse's head toward the foothills. He had no definite purpose in mind. In a dim sort of way he knew that he was hungry for a sight of Nettie. The long absence had not cured him. He loved the girl as deeply as on that first day when their eyes had met across the space of the poor "D.D.D." shack, and the laughter that had risen afterwards to their lips.

How pretty she had looked, despite her shabby dress. How her hair had shone in the sun! How gentle and good and sweet she had been to her little brothers and sisters! Even the strange woman in the C.P.R. shack had melted before Nettie's shy effort to help her. No one could have resisted Nettie, in those days, thought the unhappy Cyril, and told himself that it was small wonder that he had "fallen so hard for her." He had seen many women in the big cities of America, but he had found no face like Nettie's. No, he wouldn't change for any girl in the States *his* girl. And calling her "his" in his thought, woke him suddenly to a realization that Nettie was no longer his. Someone had cut him out! Still, he suffered such a longing again to see the girl he loved, that he thought he would risk offending her by going to Bar Q before he should bury himself in the deep woods.

On the road, a couple of riders from the hill country joined him part of the way, and their suggestive gossip only partially aroused him from his moody abstraction. It was the mention of the girl's name and the leering significance of the words that caused him to sit up abruptly, his hat pushed back, as his glance questioned the men dangerously. They protested they were only "stringing" him, and rode off swiftly. What had been hinted at was the necessity of an early marriage for the girl at Bar Q, and the assumption that he, Cyril Stanley, had come back in time.

Cyril turned this over heavily in his mind, shaking his head as if it were beyond him, but he diverted his course absently from the hill, and decided that he would go for a few days to his homestead. He would stay in the little house he had built for Nettie. He wanted to look over the place that was to have been their home. Later he would go to Bar Q. At least, Nettie would not refuse to bid him "Good-bye."

As he rode along, his hat over his eyes, smarting tears bit at his lids, and the heart of the lad who had sung on the trail and about his work was heavy as lead within him.

At the homely little cabin, somewhat of his faith and confidence in her flowed into life again. Perhaps it had all been a hideous mistake. Perhaps Nettie had been merely "mad" with him, for going to Barstairs. Well, a girl had a right to be "mad." Maybe she was over it now. There was no accounting for a girl's moods, and he "wasn't no saint," and he wouldn't hold anything against her. He'd forget all he had suffered these last cruel months, if Nettie would only smile at him once again. If she'd just look at him and speak to him as she used to do. Nettie! *His* girl! His own, out of all the world! It had been a case of love at first sight. They had often declared this, and it had been, so Nettie had said more than once, love that would never die. She had meant that when she had said it, sitting hand in hand with him in tie berry bushes, with the night sun peeping over the tops of the trees, and glistening like moonrays on the whispering leaves.

The more he locked about him at the cabin, full of the articles that Nettie herself had helped him to make, the stronger grew his hope and faith in the girl. A new excitement exhilarated him; that impulse that makes a man feel that suddenly life is worth living. He felt suddenly kindly and warmly toward the world again, and even the storm, breaking gradually over the country, and shaking the sturdy little shack, could not dampen his spirits.

He was whistling and bustling about the shack on that March day, when Dr. McDermott's bang upon the door was heard, and he opened to greet his old friend heartily and with unaffected delight in seeing him again. Dr. McDermott was associated always in his thought with Nettie. He had brought Nettie into the world! "A corking day's job, believe me," Cyril pronounced it always.

"Hello, doc. Gee, it's good to see your good old mug again. How'd you know I was back? How're you, doc?"

But his old friend was scowling at him like an angry bulldog, his underlip thrust out, and his face puckered into lines of most palpable disapproval. What is more, he was pointedly ignoring the outstretched hand of the cordial Cyril.

"No, sir, I'll not shake hands with a scallawag. Not till he's done the right thing, by gad!"

"Wow, doc! What's biting you?"

"Lad," said Dr. McDermott sternly, "I'm not here on any pleasure call upon you. I've come as a matter of duty, mon to mon, to ask— to demand—that you do the right thing by that puir lass."

"Lass! who do you mean?"

"You know damned well who I mean. None other, mon, but Nettie Day."

At the name, Cyril, already lean and haggard, turned ashen and stern.

"There are certain things I don't discuss with no man. One of them's—Nettie. I don't let no man talk to me of *her*. Some coyotes on the road stopped me and started to blab some stuff about her, but they shut up tight enough and gave me the heels of their broncos before they'd barely got started with that line of talk. And I ain't letting even an old friend like you are say anything about Nettie. What's fallen between me and her is our affair."

Dr. McDermott's fist fell heavily on the table.

"Lad, ye're going to marry that girl, if I have to shove you by your neck to the parson."

A light burst over the boy's face. His eyes widened as he stared at the doctor incredulously, and then nearly wept for joy.

"I say, that's a good joke on me. Is *that* what you are drivin' at, doc? Marry her! Say, I'd marry Nettie Day this blessed minute if she'd have me!"

"Very good, lad. You'll have your chance. I've got her now at Miss Loring's. I'll go myself after the missionary, if you'll lend me a horse. Trail's not fit for a car. I'll do my best to get back first thing in the morning. Meanwhile, you'll have a chance to get your house in shape. You'll want it to shine for that wife and baby of yours."

"That wi—and——Say, what's the joke, anyway?"

The doctor was now in better humour. His mission had been highly satisfactory, and after all, a lad was only a lad, and he liked young Cyril Stanley. There was good stuff in Cyril—good Scotch stuff at that.

Cyril, thinking that the doctor was making one of the coarse jokes of the countryside that were common enough at the time of a wedding, laughed weakly, though the words stuck in his mind queerly. To change the subject, he said:

"Doc, what do you suppose ever possessed Nettie—to treat me as she did. When I got back from Barstairs—let me see, that was last October—no, before that a bit—what does she do but run away from me, and when I chased after her, she turned me down dead cold—Said she'd changed—wasn't the same, and——a—and—she wanted me to go away—made me think some one'd cut me out with her, and—"

Cyril broke off. He was still raw from the memory of that time.

"I don't blame her a bit," blurted the doctor, with pretended wrath. "If it wasn't for that baby now, she'd be better to send you packing altogether. What's the matter with you young people to-day? Can't you hold back like respectable people? Can't you realize that even though you marry the girl now, she'll always be branded with the shame of this thing? And it's not only the lass to be considered, there's the innocent child—the baby to consider."

"That's the third or fourth time that you've said that word. What do you mean anyway? What baby? Whose?"

"Whose? Why your own, lad—yours and Nettie's."

"Mine and— Have you gone plumb crazy, doc?"

"Not I, lad. I helped bring your child into the world this morning, and Nettie's resting quiet now, and waiting for you, I have no doubt. Now, lad—"

He broke off, for something in the look and motion of Cyril Stanley stopped him from further reproach.

"I've no intention of being hard on you. Young blood is— young blood, and I was young myself once."

Cyril had staggered back, like one mortally struck. Slowly the truth had dawned upon him, and with the realization that Nettie had been false to him, something primitive and furious seemed to shake the foundations of his being; something that was made up of outrage and ungodly hatred.

"So—she's—got—a baby, has she?"

"A wee lad——"

"And you come to me—to *me*, to get a name for it!"

"To you? Who else?"

"Who else?" jeered the lad frantically. "Ask *her*."

Before the savagery of that tortured glance, Dr. McDermott retreated, and a comprehension of the truth flashed upon him. He was amazed, stunned by the thought that someone other than Cyril was responsible for the girl's downfall. Who then? Slowly he turned the matter over in his mind, rejecting one by one each of the possible men who came to his mind, till suddenly he found his mind fronted by a great sinister figure. The Bull! There grew into

131

his recollection a day at Bar Q. The evil expression on the face of the cowman, as behind his wife's back he watched Nettie Day, with his greedy, covetous eyes.

Dr. McDermott's shoulders seemed to bend as if under a load, and for a long time he scanned the furious boy before him, ere speaking in a voice that shook:

"The Lord help you, lad! The Lord help us all in our deep trouble. Give us sober and humble hearts. Teach us to bear as best we can the iniquities of the wicked who beset us. Amen."

The closing of the door acted like a spur upon Cyril Stanley. Alone with his frenzy and despair, he too looked about him, as if seeking some outlet for his feelings. There was a great axe lying hard by the door of the outkitchen. The young man grasped and whirled the thing aloft. It crashed down upon the table, splintering it in two. Again and again he wielded it, wreaking destruction upon every object in the room. With a steady, growing rage, he smashed the furniture he had bought for Nettie Day. Turning to the storeroom, he brought forth a five-gallon can of kerosene. This he deliberately poured upon the floor.

He put on his chaps, his sheepskin, fur cap and spurs, made a bundle of a few other clothes and effects, and tramped to the door. Outside, he smashed the glass panes of the windows, and a gale of snow went flying in. He struck a match, shepherded the flame, and kneeling by the door, tossed it in. It fell into a pool of kerosene.

The flames ran like a snake around the floor, leaped to the walls and the piles of broken chairs and tables, and roared to the roof. The dry logs crackled as the flames hungrily swept along the wall.

The house went up in a furious blaze. Long after Cyril Stanley had disappeared into the great timber country, the burning of his homestead rose above the blanket of snow, which was to fold the smouldering ruins under its soft weight.

CHAPTER XXI

SPRING CAME LATE TO ALBERTA THAT YEAR, and it was May before the farmers were upon the land.

Following the heavy March snowfalls, came zero weather, and the snow showed no signs of thawing till well into May.

Angela Loring was especially anxious that year to be upon her land early, for she wished to keep Nettie with her, and she had an ambitious scheme which she believed would tempt the girl to remain. Since her recovery, Nettie was waiting for the weather to break, so that she might go to Calgary in search of work. She would be unknown there, and there was a great scarcity of help in the city. Dr. McDermott had told her this. Angela, from the first day, had taken charge of the baby, and almost it seemed as if it were more her child than Nettie's. Nettie was afraid of this child of the Bull. Before the breaking of the cold spell, and while she was still weak, she would sit at the window and stare unseeingly out at the bleak prospect without. Spring is an unpleasant season in Alberta, and it was more than usually so that year. With Angela gone to the fields or the barns about her work, Nettie was thus shut in alone with her baby. Yet she made no effort to go to it, to take it in her arms or to fondle it.

Undersized and weak, it nevertheless cried little, and its weird, tiny face was curiously like that of a bird's. There was something pitifully unfinished about this child of Nettie's, though it was in no way deformed. It had simply been forced into the world before the world was ready for it, and, weak and puny, without the sustenance of the mother's breast—for Nettie was unable to nurse her child—it made slow progress. At the end of April it weighed no more than the day it was born.

If Nettie, immersed in her own cares, noted not the condition of her child, its foster mother was filled with alarm and anxiety. Dr. Mc-Dermott was no longer an unwelcome visitor at the shack. Indeed he was oftener than not sent for. Jake, often loafing about and sleeping half of the time in the deserted sheds built by Cyril, could be dispatched upon such an errand. No matter where he was, or upon what engaged, the doctor seldom failed to respond to Angela's summons. Tramping into the shack, stamping the snow off his feet, he would seem to look fiercely at the women. Always he found something to scold about; but although his words were rough, his hands were gentle as a mother's when he took the little baby in his arms. Angela watched him on these occasions with bated breath and the tense anxiety of the mother herself, while Nettie hung aloof, forcing her gaze to remain fixed steadily outdoors.

More than once, Angela Loring was very close to the man. He would look up and surprise the film before her eyes, as anxiously she watched "her" baby. To cover his own feelings, he would shortly ask her for this or that article, and she waited upon him meekly. Once, kneeling by his side, as the baby lay upon his knees, the little wan face puckered into something that Angela declared with conviction was a smile. Her delight and excitement over this caused her to put her arms about the baby on his knee, and all before she realized what was happening, she found her hand held in the doctor's close clasp. Their eyes met, and the colour slowly receded from her cheeks.

But that night she went into the bedroom, pulled to the burlap curtain between it and the outer room, and turning the articles in the box that had come with her from England, Angela Loring brought up something new in that prairie shack—a mirror—a woman's hand-mirror of ornate tortoiseshell, with a silver crest upon it. For some time she held it in her hand, face down, before she found the courage, slowly, to hold it before her face. For a long time she looked, the bright, haunted eyes slowly scanning that strange face before her, with its crown of soft grey curls. She was kneeling on the floor by her bed, and suddenly her hand fell to her lap, with the mirror in it. Angela Loring said, in a choking whisper, to the vision in the glass: "I'm an old fool! I'm an old fool!"

Her programme for that season was an ambitious one for a slight woman. She purposed to put in one hundred and fifty acres of crop, and to hay over sixty more acres. Not content with working her own land, she proposed to work and seed Cyril's. This was to be the stake that would keep Nettie with her. She felt sure that the girl would not fail to respond to this opportunity to help the man she loved. For, according to the homestead law at that time, the land had to be fenced, worked and lived upon so many years. If Cyril forsook his homestead, he stood to lose the quarter, and all the work and money already expended would go for naught. When Angela laid the proposition before Nettie, she witnessed the first excitement the girl had shown since the doctor had brought her to the ranch. She was aroused from her apathy and despair, and when Angela declared moreover that she needed help, and if Nettie would not help her, she would be obliged to employ help, something she was totally unable to afford, Nettie responded with almost fanatic zeal.

"Oh my, yes, Angel, I just wish't you'd give me the chance. I'd love to do the work. I'll do it alone if you'll let me. I'll work my fingers to the bone to—to—make up to him—and to you, Angel."

"That's all right. I'm glad you feel that way, because I need your help badly. I believe it's going to be a crop year anyway, because the snow, when it does melt, is bound to mean all sorts of moisture for the land. Meanwhile, we can do a bit of fencing. Mine need repairing badly, and so do parts of Cyril's.

We've got to cross-fence between his pasture land and where the crop is to go in. He's got quite a few head of horses and cattle running loose, I see, and they've got to be driven off the grain land. I'm going out after a couple of heavy horses of his I saw the other day on his land. I think I can corral them, and they'll come in first-rate for the plough."

"Oh, Angel, let me go. I understand horses better'n you do. It's awful hard to drive them when they've been loose like that all winter. Do let me go along."

"You'll stay right here. Look now, I'm going to run things here, and you do as you're told."

"Well, don't forget to take a halter, will you, and, Angel, you want to keep away from their hind feet—even on horse. Sometimes they kick right out. Dad was lamed that way, drivin' in wild horses. Got kicked while on horseback, right in the shin. My, it was awful!"

"I'm all right. Don't you worry about me," said Angela. "Mind the baby while I'm gone, and look here, if he cries, there's barley gruel in that bottle. Heat it, standing it in hot water—but not too hot. I think he'll be all right till I get back."

Nettie did a curious thing after Angela left her alone that day. She went over to the rough cot that Angela had made for the baby, out of a grocery box, and for a long time she stood looking down at the small sleeping face. Then, almost unconsciously, her hand hovered above the tiny one of her baby. It opened and closed snugly about the girl's fingers, and at that warm contact something overwhelming burst into being in her heart. It was as if tentacles had reached out and fastened about her heart. That little curled up fist fairly burned her with its appeal and reproach. Nettie drew her hand fiercely away, and ran wildly into the adjoining room. With her breath coming and going tumultuously, she cried:

"I don't want to love him! I don't want to. He's *him*, and I wish't I'd died before I—I—come to this."

Seeking for some physical outlet on which to vent her pent-up feelings, she looked about her. A pair of scissors lay on Angela's dressing table, and this Nettie seized. She could not tell why, at that moment, she found herself slashing into her long hair. The big braids dropped to the floor with a soft thud. Nettie was shorn of her beautiful hair; but she was by no means disfigured. In a way, her childlike, simple beauty was almost enhanced by the short hair, which accentuated her extreme youth and simplicity of nature; but when Angela, coming in, stopped on the threshold and stared at her condemningly, Nettie knew that she had offended her friend.

"Nettie Day, what you have done is an act of sheer vandalism," said the woman, who had herself cut to the scalp her own hair.

"Oh, Angel, I wanted to be like you. I didn't want no more to be like a woman——"

Angela's face blanched.

"So I'm not like a woman, then?"

"I didn't mean that, Angel. You're more like a woman in your heart than anyone I ever knew, 'cept Mrs. Langdon, and I just wanted to make myself so that—so that no one would ever want to look at me again. Just's if I was same as a man and——"

"And I suppose you think you've succeeded," said Angela dryly. "Never fear. It will take more than the cutting of your hair to keep men from you, Nettie Day. However, it's your own hair, and I suppose you meant all right. They say 'Hell is paved with good intentions.' But you needn't think that because I—was fool enough to—to—make a freak of myself, that I approve of you or anyone else doing it."

"I'm sorry, Angel. I'm awfully sorry. I—I want to be as much like you as I can be. I want to wear them men's overalls too and do——"

"As far as the overalls go, that's all right. *They're* sensible; but look here, Nettie, don't let me catch you doing anything like that to disfigure yourself again, and don't you go slashing any more into your hair. It doesn't look bad now, but even you would look a fright if you had cut it as I did—right to the scalp."

"It's growing in now, and it looks—right pretty, Angel," said Nettie wistfully. "D'you know, you ain't nearly as ugly as you think you are," added Nettie with girlish *naïveté*, which brought a chuckle from Angela, warming the baby bottle at the stove.

They began to fence in mid-April. The ground was hard, and without proper hole diggers they were at a further disadvantage. However, Angela said she did not want to waste any time on repairing fences, once the land was ready for the crop. Cyril's quarter was already fairly well fenced, but the dividing line between the two quarters had never been completed. However, as the two places were now to be worked as one, there was no need of constructing the line fence. Persisting at this, their first task of the season, they achieved an inadequate protection for the proposed crop. This uneven line of barbed wire, set on wavering posts, aroused the derisive condemnation of Dr. McDermott, who warned them that cattle would have no trouble in breaking through; that the two wires did not constitute a legal fence, the requirement being three. Angela, more than ever stiff and cold in her attitude toward the doctor in those days, rejoined that "they would take their chances this year."

The herd law was now in force, and it was against the law for cattle to be at large on the road or road allowances in that particular part of the country. The doctor grouchily warned them that that concerned stray cattle, but there was absolutely nothing to prevent a herd driven by riders going through. Nothing, returned Angela indignantly, except the fact that most reputable riders had a professional sense of honour, so far as other people's grain fields were concerned, and she knew none that would be likely to turn driven cattle into a grain field. Such things were not done in a country like Alberta. Besides, cattle were unlikely to be moved in the summer time, and by the fall, the harvest would be in, and the grain safe.

"Have it your way," returned the doctor. "If you will do a mon's work, do it in a mon's way." This gratuitous advice was treated in the disdainful silence it deserved.

They had before them a truly gigantic task, the putting in of over one hundred and fifty acres of grain—flax, barley, oats, wheat, green feed and rye.

As soon as the land was in condition to be worked, they were upon it. For days they had been sorting over and mending harnesses and bridles, sharpening the implements and getting everything ready into shape. Eight work-horses had been brought up from the pasture, and for a few days had been fed on oats and given special care. Nettie by this time was strong, and she knew farm work and was at home with horses, so that she was of invaluable assistance to the less experienced, if self-reliant, Angela.

The baby went into the field with them, carried in a large box. Here among its pillows, Nettie's child slept in blissful unconsciousness of the tragedy of his existence. In the latter weeks, he had been gaining somewhat, and his blue, wandering eyes more than once had smiled up at the adoring Angela. She needed not now to imagine every contortion of the little face to be a smile, for she could bring a smile easily to the baby's face, by the single expedient of chirping.

Nettie went on the plough, the hardest of the implements to ride. There had been some argument between the girls as to which implement each should ride, Angela contending that Nettie was hardly in fit condition to stand the rough shaking on the plough; but Nettie stubbornly insisted that she felt "strong as an ox," and that she had ridden the plough since she was a little girl. "Dad put me into the field when I was just ten," she told Angela. "You know Dad couldn't afford to stay home and work our quarter, because our land was so poor, and he had to go out on other farms to make wages, because we were such a hungry family, and it took sights of food to fill us all."

So Nettie rode the plough, and then the disc. Angel was on the harrow and the seeder. She only gave in about the plough because Nettie pointed out that the seeder required brains, and that, the girl sadly admitted, she lacked. She had never seeded, even at home. Dad had always come back in time todothat. Angel, feeling the importance of her two seasons' experience in seeding, argued no further. She seeded six inches deep, a precautionary measure, so she told Nettie, against a dry year. The weather favoured them. Intermittent rains and flurries of snow kept the ground damp enough for fertilization, but not too wet for sowing. Nevertheless, said Angela, you never could tell about Alberta's climate. Drought might start with June, and then where would the careless farmers be?

During this period, at least, somewhat of Nettie's cares were allayed. Labouring from five in the morning till sundown will do much to exhaust a body and mind, and intent upon doing first-rate work, her mind was for the first time jerked from a contemplation of her troubles.

The preparation of the ground and the seeding done, there were a few weeks' interval, when they brought to the corrals their few head of stock and themselves branded, dehorned and vaccinated them against blackleg. Nettie then went over to Cyril's quarter with the plough, and broke new land, a task by no means easy, since the ground was rough virgin soil, and in many places there were rocks and bushes and tree stumps. Meanwhile, Angela summer-fallowed on her own quarter.

July came in on a wave of intense heat. There was haying to be done on Cyril's quarter. Angel's fields had been over-pastured, and she proposed to let them lie fallow for that year. The two girls put up seventy-five tons of hay. Angela was upon the rake, an easy implement to ride. Nettie was on the mower. Then Angela ascended the buck, and Nettie did the stacking. As the big golden pile grew from day to day under their hands, they felt a tremendous pride and satisfaction in their work. There was something to show for it this year, Angela declared, and her faith was pinned upon a sure crop—her first since coming to Alberta.

Before and after their field work, they had considerable chores and housework to do. Nettie milked, cared for the sitting hens and spring chicks, looked after the great sow with her litter of spring piggies; she watered and fed the horse and cleaned the barns and stables. Meanwhile, Angela prepared the meals, made the butter, cleaned the house, and took full charge of the baby.

In Nettie's avoidance of her child there was fear rather than aversion. The child of the man she hated, which had been forced upon her, aroused in her breast strange tumults. At the thought of its father she shuddered, and told herself that she hated what was his; but there were times when melting, passionate impulses consumed her, and then it was all she could do to restrain her arms from seizing her baby and holding it closely to her breast.

As she sat through the long day on the hard seat of the implement, rocking and shaking from side to side, as she drove her four-horse team over the rough land, Nettie tried to keep her mind upon her work. Guiding her horses expertly, making a clean, workmanlike job of which even a man might not have been ashamed, she sought comfort in the thought that she was working for Cyril Stanley. Yet, as the implement swept around the field, and passed on each round near that box by the straw stack where slept the baby, a great lump never failed to tighten in her throat, and her bosom rose and fell.

The harvest was close at hand, and for the first time since she had come to Alberta, Angela Loring was to have a crop.

Billowing waves of golden wheat, going forty |or more bushels to the acre, lay spread before her: barley glistening and silver, oats as tall as a man, and richly thick. The grain seemed alive, full of vitality and health. With the soft swish of the wind upon it, it stirred and murmured drowsily under the warm breath of the sun, as if chanting:

"Come, we are waiting to be reaped! Gather us in, before the cold breath of the northland shall shiver across the land, and sap our strength with its icy touch."

Of an evening, their labour in the field done, the women who had put in that crop, would walk slowly through the grain, and the soft slush of the stalks as they made a pathway through the thick growth seemed like a whisper of peace in the quiet evening. The harvest moon hung miraculously like a great orange ball above the fields; the distances seemed illimitable across the prairie land; the far horizons disappeared into a miracle of vaguely white hills, that were sketched across a sky upon which the most beautiful sunset in the world lingered nightly in lordly splendour.

They talked little, these two women; for the one was shy and reticent by nature, and the other had acquired the habit of reticence and brevity of speech. Yet each felt and understood the thought of the other, as they looked across at the moving grain.

CHAPTER XXII

THERE WAS HAIL IN THE SOUTH; hail further west; hail zig-zagged across the country, whipping down the tall grain and pelting lumps as big as eggs upon the ground, breaking windows and thumping in vindictive fury upon all in its path. The grain cringed and shivered down to the ground. A black ugly cloud, looking like a gigantic hand, was in the sky, and wherever its fingers reached out the hail fell. Not a field that it touched but was bitten to the ground; yet its course was strangely eccentric. It leaped over whole municipalities, and spat its venom down upon selected places. With troubled eyes, the girls had watched the path of the mad cloud, and knew the destructive force that was wreaking havoc over the grain lands. Nettie prayed—prayed to the God of which she knew so pitifully little, but whom Mrs. Langdon had been so near—and she asked that their fields might be spared, not hers, but Angel's and Cyril's.

The rural line rattled all of that day and evening, as excited farmers called to each other.

"Were you struck?"

"Yes, wiped out."

"Insured?"

"Not a red cent."

"Gosh, I'm sorry. There's not a spear left in my field either, but I got $10.00 on the acre."

"Think they'll allow you one hundred per cent. loss?"

"Sure they will."

"Hm! Betchu you'll thresh just the same."

The bang of a hanging up receiver.

A buzzing on the lines. All parties "listening in," gloating or commiserating over each other's misfortune.

How about Smithers?

"Say, his fields aren't touched."

"You don't say! Isn't it the devil how them hailstorms skip and miss?"

"Munson's got wiped off the map. So did Homan."

"Pederson's ain't touched even."

"Trust them Swedes to have the luck every time."

"Did you hear about Bar Q?"

"No, what?"

"Never heard they got it hardest of all? My land! There isn't a field the hail didn't get. The whole three thousand acres on the grain ranch. I see where his nibs won't do much threshing this year."

"He should worry. You can bet your bottom dollar he's got double insurance on his crop, and, say, anyway, he'll have a sight of green feed for his cattle. They say he's short of hay in the hill country this year. I'll bet he cuts the hailed stuff for feed."

"I wouldn't wonder!"

And so on.

Nettie and Angela's crops were among those few that escaped untouched. When the storm had passed and the sun blazed out upon the battered fields, there strong and sturdy, shining in the new light, the grain they had sown seemed to smile on them and call aloud to be reaped without further delay.

It was now mid-August, and the grain was ripe. Angela rode the binder, a picturesque implement with canvas wings, which when in operation resembles a sort of flying machine. Nettie followed on foot, stooking. This was a man's job, for the sheaves of grain were heavy, and it was no easy matter to bend and grasp the thick bundles and stack them in stacks; but Nettie was strong and willing and she even tried to keep up with the binder, running to the stacks, till Angel stopped her horses abruptly and refused to go on with the work unless Nettie took her time about the stooking.

The harvest occupied three weeks, but at last there came a day when the grain was all stacked. Danger of frost, hail and drought was now over. Nothing remained to be done but the threshing. Under the mellow light that suffuses the Alberta country at this time of year, in the evening, the girls rode in from their last day of harvesting. They had gleaned bravely and well.

Sound carries far in the prairie country, and from eight miles off from their ranch they could clearly hear the buzz of the threshing machine, droning like a comforting bee, at work even at night. In a few days the threshers would "pull in" to Angela's ranch; the harvested grain would be poured into the temporary granaries that they had constructed from a portion of the barn.

As they stood in the twilight, looking across at the harvest field, though they did not and perhaps could not have expressed their thoughts in words, they knew that they had produced a picture out there in the sun that was a masterpiece which no mere brush could ever catch. And as this thought came, perhaps to both of the girls, their eyes met, and they smiled warmly at each other. They turned reluctantly from the field. Nettie, glancing toward the hills, saw what looked like the shadow of a horseman silhouetted across the horizon. At first, as he came suddenly to the top of the grade, she did not recognize him, but as he rode nearer, she was shaken with an ungovernable agitation.

"Angel! Look—look—look—it's—the Bull! Oh—h!"

"You have nothing to fear, Nettie. Nettie!"

"Oh, Angel, he's come for me! I knowed he would come. I've been looking for him, dreading he would come, and now he's here. Oh, what am I to do! Where can I hide?"

Her glance went hither and thither, as it had gone that night when the Bull had trapped her in her room, and she listened like a mad person to the breaking down of her door. But now her glance was over the wide-spreading country, and before her lay the great grain stooks, which she herself had piled together. She broke from Angela's grasp and fled across the field, darting from one stack to another, and desperately crouching down behind the farthest.

Angela made no movement to stop the fleeing girl. Her eyes slightly closing, to make sure that the approaching rider was indeed Bull Langdon, she quietly went into the house. First she put the child in the basket in the inner room. Then she took down her rifle—that rifle concerning which the country people had joshed, but whose bite some of them had felt. Angela did not load it while in the house, but slowly and calmly, as Bull Langdon rode up.

CHAPTER XXIII

IT IS NOT DIFFICULT IN A COUNTRY LIKE ALBERTA for one to disappear, if he so desires. This is especially true of the ranching country.

Nettie was several months with Angela Loring before her presence there was discovered. On one side of Angela's quarter was a municipality of open range; on the other, Cyril Stanley's quarter section. Beyond Cyril's ranch was bush country that ran for several miles to the Elbow River, then out between the South and North side of the country that led up to the foothills, fifty miles out of which was the Bar Q hill ranch. Further out still was the beginning of the dense timber land, in the heart of which, on the banks of the Elbow and Bow rivers, was the Bow Claire Lumber Camp. Still beyond this, the foothills continued, growing higher and higher till they merged into the chain of Rocky Mountains.

The talk concerning Nettie Day had centred about the foothill ranching country. Her story, in fact, had run from ranch to ranch, and the general verdict was expressed in the usual country sentence: "I never would have believed it," or "I told you so." However, Nettie had disappeared from the foothills, and curiosity in a ranching country soon vanishes. Moreover, the death of Mrs. Langdon had given another morsel for excitement and exclamation to the ranch people, and after this had passed, only an occasional reference as to Nettie's whereabouts was heard.

New cares and new interests at this time were more or less concerning or harassing the country people of Alberta. There might, even as early as the spring, have been noted a certain restlessness, an apprehension, and, in some cases, positive fear. Strange stories were percolating into the ranches of sickness in the cities—sickness the nature of which was suppressed by the authorities, and diagnosed as something else, to avert a possible panic. The ranch people stuck closely to their homes that spring and summer, and they were not cordial to strangers or the usual visitor from the city—the insurance, real estate men, the drug man, and the sly, affable stranger, who winked when he sold the hands Pain Killer—"paper collar dudes" all the farm folk named them; but they as well as the motor hoboes and camp tramps who came to the ranch-houses with their ingenuous requests for anything from milk to a night's lodging, were unwelcome this summer, for the ranch people were shrewd enough to appreciate the fact that the plague could be carried to them through such mediums as these. They stuck close to home that spring and summer, and although the papers had scarehead stories of the fearful scourge in the east, Alberta believed or hoped it would prove immune.

In Yankee Valley, no one knew that the girl from the D.D.D. had returned; or that, with her child, she had found a refuge in the home of the Englishwoman.

Thus, undisturbed, and at a considerable distance from the main road and trails, Nettie found a true sanctuary at Angela Loring's ranch. Then one day, Batt Leeson, who had taken Cyril's place at the Bull camp, riding by Cyril's quarter *en route* to the foothills, paused at the sight of a girl, clad in a man's blue overalls, driving a six-horse plough team over new breaking.

Nettie, at a pause in the harvesting, when they had to wait for a field of oats to ripen, was filling in the time by breaking new land on Cyril's quarter.

Batt, jaw dropped and eyes squinting, could not believe that he saw aright. To make doubly sure, he rode close to the fence line, and from behind the shelter of a tree he waited for the plough to make its next round about the field. On and on it came, its dull rumble and clatter of iron accentuated by the stillness of the prairie. Over a piece of rising ground came

Nettie Day upon the implement. Her head was bare and the sun, glistening upon it, turned it to a ruddy gold, so that it seemed like a light, a halo above her. It had been cut to her ears, like a boy's, and the slight wind lifted and blew the hair back from her flushed face as she rode along.

"Well, I'll be switched," said the ranch hand.

He was, in fact, literally overjoyed by the discovery. It was a rich morsel of news that he would have to carry now to the foothills. "That there girl who'd got into trouble at the Bar Q was working on the land of the fellow—" Batt stopped there, chuckling and gloating. Once Cyril Stanley had punched his face for a much slighter thing than mentioning his (Cyril's) name in connection with a girl, and Batt bit his tongue upon the name of the man whom he suspected was responsible for Nettie Day's downfall.

Nettie's gaze was bent straight ahead. She did not turn or look at the rider watching her from the trail.

Things had been going from bad to worse at Bar Q. More than the usual number of calves had died from blackleg, and a number of first-class heifers had perished in the woods where the larkspur (poison weed) grew wild. A Government veterinary surgeon, after a hurried survey of such of the cattle as were on the home range, had put a blanket quarantine on all of them. This prevented their removal for months—until, in fact, the "vet" should have given them a clean bill of health.

In his absence, the cowman's stock and ranch had been badly neglected. Cattle were at large; fences out of repair; there was a careless mixing of all grades of cattle. Things were at sixes and sevens, and according to the cattleman, not "a stitch of work" had been done during his absence. One of his first "acts" was to fire all hands at the foothill ranch. This meant an entirely new outfit, and the new outfit proved worse than the old. These also were sent packing.

The constant coming of new hands to the ranch had a demoralizing effect upon the place, and with the scarcity of good help to be had at this time, and wages that went as high as $100 a month and board, Bull Langdon had his hands full at Bar Q.

He was in a chronically evil humour in these days, and he found nothing about the place that suited him. The big ranch house itself got upon his nerves. His wife had been a born home-maker, and she made the ranch house a place of comfort to which even the Bull was not insensible. She had catered to his appetite and to his whims. He had become used to the comfort and care of women; was, in fact, almost dependent upon the services he had so roughly rewarded in the past. He could not accustom himself to the empty house; nor could he endure the meals at the cook car.

He slept in these days on the ground floor of the house, in the dining-room. Where before was a room fairly shining with cleanliness and order, now boots, rough coats and trousers, shirts, and the paraphernalia of riding of the cattleman strewed the entire place, while the unmade bed, the unwashed pots and pans, the dirt upon the floor from muddy boots, and the dust of many days, gave it an atmosphere of utter filth.

Yet the Bull would never sleep upstairs since his wife's death. Her door remained closed. Nettie's, too, hung on its broken hinges, and sometimes on a windy night the knocking of that door, screeching and swinging upon its single hinge, was too much for the overwrought cattleman, and he would tramp out to the bunk-house and sleep there in preference. But he wanted his home back, and like a spoiled child whose favourite toy had been taken from him, he raged and bawled for the return of it.

He had come in from a hard day of riding, and his temper was at its worst. His enraged glance sweeping the cheerless and disordered room, his thoughts, as always, turned to the girl whom he believed belonged there. She had been gone long enough. He had put up with enough of her d——nonsense. It was time to round her up. Nettie was to him a stray head of stock that had slipped from under the lariat noose and was wandering in strange pastures. True she was a prized head, but all the more the Bull determined again to capture her. He considered that she was his personal stuff; something he had branded, and he was not a man to part with that which was his. Doggedly repeatedly, he asserted to himself that Nettie was his. He had bought her with the rest of her dad's old truck.

Batt Leeson, riding in from Barstairs, brought him the first news of the girl that he had not seen since the night of her departure.

"Say, boss, who d'you suppose I seen when I rode by Yankee Valley."

"How the h——should I know?"

"Well, I seen that Day girl that used to work up here."

Bull Langdon, twisting long strips of cowhide about a lump of lead, in the making of a bull-whip, stopped short, and his glance shot up at the slowly chewing, slowly talking ranch hand.

"What's that you say?"

"I was sayin' that I seen her—Nettie Day—over to Yankee Valley; and where'd you suppose she's livin'? Say, she must be tied up now to that Stanley fellow, because I seen her on his land and——"

"That's a damned lie!" shouted the cattle-man, and dashed the leaded cowhide to the floor with a fouler oath. Batt, his knees shaking with terror, retreated before the advance of the enraged cowman.

"It's true as God what I'm tellin' you. I seen her with my own eyes. She was breakin' land on Stanley's quarter."

Bull Langdon's eyes were bloodshot and inflamed. His face twitched hideously.

"That young scrub's at Bow Claire. His homestead's burned to the ground. You can't come to me with no such tale as that."

"B—b-b-b——but I tell you she's workin' his land. I seen her. I stopped right close and looked her over to make sure. I ain't makin' no mistake. Thought at first I might be, 'cause I figure that a girl in her condition——"

"Whatcha mean by her condition?"

"Sa-ay, boss." Batt scratched his head, uncertain whether to proceed; itching to tell the tale of the girl's fall, but fearing that menacing spark in the eyes of the man glaring at him. "I thought you knew."

"Knew what?"

"'Bout her condition."

Batt essayed a sly, ingratiating wink, but it had no placating effect upon the man before him.

"I don't know what the devil you're talking about."

"Gosh, boss, everyone knows 'bout Nettie Day. She's a-goin' to have a baby—mebbe she's got it now. I expect she has."

"What-t!"

The Bull's eyes bulged. A huge wave of unholy joy was racing through his being.

A baby! His! His! His own! His and that gell's!

He threw back his head and burst into a torrent of laughter. His wild mirth shook the beams and the rafters of the old ranch house, and seemed to reverberate about the entire place.

"Well, by G——" said the cowman, and reached for his riding boots. He pulled them on with a vim, chuckling and chortling, and pausing now and then to smack his hip.

"Goin' ridin', boss?"

"You betchur life I am."

"Where you goin'?"

"I'm goin' to round up," said Bull Langdon, smacking his lips.

"After some loose stock?"

"A pure bred heifer with a calf at heel," said Bull Langdon. "They've got my brand on them."

CHAPTER XXIV

BY THE DOOR OF HER SHACK THE ENGLISHWOMAN STOOD, her rifle in hand, coolly raising her head to stare at the blustering cowman, who had dismounted, and, fists on hips, was standing before her. For the first time in his life Bull Langdon faced a woman who did not fear him. Her cold, unwavering glance travelled over him, from his hun-like head down to his great, ugly feet, and back with cool disparagement, straight into his quailing eyes.

"You seen anything of that gell, Nettie Day?"

Angela disdained to answer. Her glance was above his head, and presently she said:

"Will you kindly remove yourself from my place? I don't want you here."

"You don't, heh? Well, I'm here to get something of my own. Do you get me?"

"Oh, yes, I get you all right; but you'll take nothing off *my* place, you may be sure of that."

He stood his ground with bravado, and blurted out his demand. He had come for Nettie. He intended to have her and his kid. She belonged to him; was his "gell," and he had bought her just as he had her "dad's old truck." He'd have been over before this, but his cattle had tied him down since his return from the States, and he "wasn't the kind of man to neglect his cattle for a woman."

As he spoke, the woman's level gaze continued coolly upon him, as if his blustering outburst, while it concerned her in no way, nevertheless aroused her amused contempt. But when he made a motion as if to enter the house, Angela Loring slowly brought her rifle to her shoulder and took deadly aim at the man before her. Across the length of the rifle's barrel her eye squinted straight at him. He jumped back when he saw that curled finger at the trigger.

"What the h——you tryin' to do?"

She spoke from the end of her rifle, and still aimed unwaveringly at him.

"You clear off my place! You enter my house and I'll shoot you down with less compunction that I would a dog."

He slouched a few paces further back, a nasty laugh breaking from him. At his horse's side his bravado returned to him.

"Guess there ain't goin' to be no trouble gettin' what's my own. The law's on my side. I've as much right to that kid, that's my own stuff, as the gell has."

"Oh, have you?" said Angela coolly. "Unfortunately for you the child is no longer even Nettie's. It's mine. She gave me the child for adoption."

"She hadn't no right to do that," said the Bull, in an overpowering rage at this intelligence. "It ain't hers only. It ain't hers to give away."

"Oh, isn't it though?"

"No, it ain't, and I'll show you a thing or two. There won't be no funny business with guns neither when a couple of mounties come up here after what's mine."

"I wouldn't talk about the law, if I were you. You see, when you committed that crime against Nettie, she was a minor in law. I don't know how many years in the penitentiary that may mean for you. Her lawyers will know."

He had blanched and turned a sickening grey at the word "penitentiary." Nettie's youth had not occurred to him.

"——and then," went on the Englishwoman, "apart from the legal aspects of the case, I wonder that you take a chance in a country like this. Consider what may happen to you if the truth about Nettie becomes known in this ranching country. We have an unwritten law of our own in such cases, you know, and those who do know about Nettie have been blaming an innocent boy. What will they say—what will they do, when they know that the most hated and detested man in the country attacked a young defenceless girl when she was alone in his house? I wouldn't care to be in your shoes when *that* fact leaks out, as you may be sure it will. I'll take care of that! You can trust me to denounce you without measure!"

The Bull shouted, purple with rage:

"There ain't no man livin' I'm afraid of, an' there ain't no man in the country strong enough to beat me."

"I don't doubt that. You look as if you might have the strength of a gorilla; but then where a hand will not serve, a rope will, and you know it will be short work for your own men to hang you to a tree when young Cyril Stanley ropes you. Now I've talked to you enough. You get off my place, or I'll put a shot in that ugly fist of yours that'll lame you for the rest of your days."

He was on horse, and she laughed at his hurry, but as he rode off, the venomous expression on his face turned her heart cold with a new fear, and his words:

"So long, old hen, you'll sing another tune when we meet again."

CHAPTER XXV

"JAKE, I WANT YOU TO RIDE LIKE 'HELL ON FIRE' to Springbank, where you'll find Dr. McDermott. Ask at the post office for him, and you may meet him on the trail. Don't spare Daisy, even if you have to kill her riding. Leave her at Springbank to rest up and come back with the Doc. And, Jake, if you get back by tomorrow night, I'll—I'll give you a whole pound of brown sugar and a can of molasses. Now skedaddle, and for God's sake, don't fail us."

"Me go! Me fly on the air!" cried the breed exultantly. Without saddle or bridle—merely a halter rope, Jake was on the Indian bronco, and was off like a flash on the trail.

Angela masked her fears to the white and trembling Nettie.

"Nothing to worry about," she said carelessly. "He's afraid of my gun, Nettie, the big coward!"

"Oh, Angel, I'm not afraid for myself, but for the baby. He's a terrible man when he's in a passion, and he never gives up nothing that's his."

"But you're not his," said Angel sharply, "and neither is the baby. He's mine. You said I could have him, and I won't give him up."

"Oh, Angel, I don't want you to. He's better with you than anyone else, and although I do love him"—Nettie's voice was breaking piteously—"yet there are times when I *can't* forget that he is the Bull's."

"He's not—he's all yours, Nettie. There's not a trace of that wild brute in our baby. I don't see how you can ever think it. Just look at the darling," and she held the laughing, fair-haired baby out in her arms. It was now at the crowing age, and the daily outdoor life in the field had done much to give him the health and strength he had lacked at birth. He had Nettie's eyes and hair, and unlike his mother's seriousness, her baby was always laughing and gurgling aloud his happy contentment with life.

Nettie looked at him with swimming eyes.

"He *is* sweet!" she said in a choking voice, and kneeling beside Angel, on whose lap the baby lay, she put her head down upon her child.

Jake did not return the following evening, nor the night after that. Though each sought to hide the fact from the other, they kept a constant lookout along the trail, and their ears were strained for the comforting sound of the motor, which on a still day could sometimes be heard while two or even three miles from the ranch.

They would have left the ranch, but for the fact that the threshers were due to come within a few days, and it would have been ruinous to Angel at this time not to be threshed while the machine was on the way past their ranch. Once the threshing was done, and the grain safely stored in the granary, or sold directly to a commission man, who had already called upon Angela, they would be free to make a trip to Calgary, and there seek counsel and protection.

Meanwhile, each night they bolted and barricaded their door. The baby between them, they lay on either side of the bed, armed. They slept but little. Wide-eyed, in the darkness of the night, these women kept their vigil, each hoping that the other slept.

On the third night, toward morning, Nettie started up with a cry. She had heard something moving without the shack. Their hands gripped upon their rifles; they sat up in the dark, listening intently. Then Angela declared that it was only the wind, and Nettie said:

"It sounds like thunder, doesn't it. Maybe we're goin' to have another storm."

"Let it storm," said Angela, glad of the other's voice in the dark. "Our crop's harvested, and no hail can hurt us now. Is the light still going in the kitchen?"

"Yes." After a moment Nettie said:

"I ain't afraid of nothing now for myself, but I don't want nothing to happen to you or my baby."

"My baby, you mean," corrected Angela, pretending to laugh. Nevertheless, her arm drew the little baby close to her side, and she felt a thrill that was all mother.

After another long, tense pause, when they imagined things stirring about the place:

"Let's talk," said Angela suddenly. "I can't sleep and neither can you, and we never do talk much."

"I expect that's because we've always had to work most o' the time," said Nettie. "Isn't it queer that you and me should be such friends?"

"Why queer?"

"I'm what they call 'scrub stock'—and you——"

"So'm I—scrub. That's the kind worth being. The common clay, Nettie. The other kind is shoddy and false and——"

"Oh, Angel, I think you are just sweet and good."

"I'm not sweet and good," said Angel stoutly. "There's nothing heroic about me."

"I don't care what you are," said Nettie, "I'll always love you. Sometimes when I get thinking of how hard everything's been for me in this life, then I think of you and Mrs. Langdon, and I say to myself: 'You're a lucky girl, Nettie!' Not everybody in the world has got a friend, have they, Angel?"

"No—very few of us have," said Angel sadly. "Nettie, did you hear that?"

"What?"

"It sounded like—like a moan. Listen!"

In the dark stillness of the night, a long, low bawl was repeated.

"It's cattle," said Nettie.

"Sure that's what it is?"

"Oh yes, I know their calls, though I didn't know there was any near us."

"Passing along the trail probably. It's getting toward the fall, you know."

"Angel, do you believe in God?"

"No—that is, in a way I do. Do you?"

"Yes. Mrs. Langdon used to say that God was in us—in our hearts. He can't be in every heart, can he?"

"Why not?"

"Well, Bull Langdon's, for instance. God *couldn't* abide in *his* heart, could He?"

"No, I should think not."

"But Mrs. Langdon believed it. She used to say that God loved him as well as any of us, but that Bull was 'in error,' and that some day God would open his eyes, and then he would be powerful good."

"Hm! He'd have to open his eyes pretty wide, I'm thinking," said Angel. "But try and sleep now, Nettie. I'm feeling a bit drowsy myself. Maybe we can snatch a wink or two before morning. Good-night, Nettie."

"Good-night, Angel. I think it's true. God *is* in our hearts. I believe it."

"I believe He's in yours, anyway," said Angela softly. "Good-night, old girl."

But God dwelt not in the heart of Bull Langdon. Under the silvering light of the moon, magically tinting the sleeping land, and across the shining valley, came the cowman. He was driving a great herd of steers. Penned in corrals for shipment to the Calgary stockyards, they had been left unfed for two days, and now they came down the hill eagerly and impatiently, seeking the withheld food.

The Bull, behind the herd on his huge bay mare, drove them before him at a rapid pace, whirling and cracking his long bull whip above their heads. The Banff highway was bare. He chose the gritty roads, and heads down, the hungry steers nosed the bare ground, till they came to the level lands, and turned into the road allowances between the farms. The grain fields, odorous of cut hay and grain, but added to the torture and hunger of the maddened steers, who moaned and sniffed as they were driven unwillingly along.

All of the day and most of the night they travelled without pause. In the first grey of the dawn they came before the frail fences of the Lady Angela Loring. Down went the two lines of barbed wire that the women had insecurely set up, before the impetuous stampede of the wild cattle.

When Angela and Nettie stepped from out their shack that morning, and looked with amazement at the vindictive work of Bull Langdon, the road was still grey with the raised dust of the departing animals, turning off the road allowance for the main trail, the Bar Q brand flashing on their left ribs. Filled to the neck with the reaped grain, they rolled along the way to Calgary.

Before their barren fields now stood the two girls, overwhelmed by the magnitude of the disaster that had befallen them. They said not a word to each other, but Angela, like one grown suddenly old, turned blindly to the house, while Nettie threw herself down blindly upon the ground and burst into bitter tears.

Her work-hardened, tough little hands fallen loosely by her side, by that poor home-made table of rough wood, Angela tried to figure a way out of the appalling problem now facing her. The money on her implements, bought on the instalment plan, was due; she owed the municipality for her seed; a chattel mortgage was on her stock. That crop would have wiped out all of her obligations.

In other years a crop failure had been met by her work at the Bar Q, and a bit of money earned from eggs and butter; but now she had not merely herself to consider. There were two other living souls wholly dependent upon her. To the desolate woman, hungry and broken of heart, Nettie and her baby were nearer and dearer to her than herself.

Nettie, in the meanwhile, scarce knowing what she was doing, wandered out into the fields, where the destroyed stooks told the cruel tale of their appalling loss.

She was recalled by someone pulling at her sleeve, and looking up saw the half-breed, Jake. He was kneeling beside her, holding out a little bunch of buttercups. Nettie tried to smile through her tears, and she took the flowers gratefully.

"Thank you, Jake. My! they're pretty!"

A tear rolled down her cheek and splashed upon the buttercups. Jake saw it, and his eyes grew alarmed.

"Nettie! You cry! Why you cry? What for you make a cry on your eye?"

"Don't mind me, Jake. I'm just—just foolish, that's all. Where'd you come from?"

"Jake come out in notermobile with Doctor. Big ride— run like wind on road. Doc's at house. He eat. Jake got a hungry too."

"Well, you go up to the house. Angel will give you something too."

He hesitated, searching her face with troubled wonderment, his brows puckered. As though, with pain, the poor fellow sought some solution to the problem of Nettie's tears.

"What's matter, Nettie? Why you make a cry? *Him* hurt Nettie again, yes?"

"Oh yes, Jake—again." Her lip quivered, and again a big tear rose and fell. The half-breed's face flamed savagely.

"The Bull! Him no good. Jake kill 'im some day sure!"

He made a curiously savage motion with his arms, and Nettie shook her head, trying to smile reprovingly.

In the house, Dr. McDermott broke from his Scotch habit of reticence into a volume of fluent, angry speech. He had met the Bar Q herd along the road, and as he drove by

Angela's fields realized the disaster that had befallen them. Her first words apprised him of the fact that his suspicions were correct. She said:

"Bull Langdon turned his steers into my crop. He has ruined us."

Thumping down in the seat opposite her, he tried to arouse her from her crushed condition of mind by banging upon the table, and promising "to beat the mon to pulp" the first time he should meet him. Angela regarded him strangely. There was something piteously beaten about that look.

"No—you shan't mix up with him, doctor. It wouldn't do any good now."

"A mon like that should be hung," raged the doctor. "He's a menace to a decent community—an enemy to the race."

After a while, Angela said:

"Dr. McDermott, I'm through. I can't go on—fighting. I'm beaten!"

"Through! Beat!" roared her friend—he who had preached so violently against her labouring as a man. "Why, lass, you've only just begun. You're of a fighting race, and you'll not go down. You're not of the breed to admit you're beat."

She said sadly:

"A lot you know of my—breed."

Dr. McDermott thrust out his chin, fixed her with his angry glare and said:

"There's no one knows more of you and your—breed—than I."

She glanced up at that, troubled and slightly startled, though her face paled and stiffened, as it always did at the recollection of her past. The doctor went on, regardless of her shrinking:

"Don't you remember the lad you whipped because he'd not let you ride the young Spitfire? Don't you remember the lad that twenty-four years ago your father sent to college in Glasgow?"

Slowly her eyes brightened with excitement. Colour touched her cheeks. He had shot her back into the mists of a memory in the past that was not cruel, and that did not make her wince with the mere pain of memory. She continued to stare at him in that dumb, bright way, searching the rough face before her in an effort to discover the familiar, freckled friendly one of the boy she had stolen out many a time as a child to play with. It seemed incredible that he should be the Scotch doctor, her one true friend in Canada.

"Take back the money," he pleaded huskily, "that your father spent for making a doctor of a stable lad. You'll let me stake you, will you not, lass?"

Unexpectedly her eyes filled and brimmed over. Even as Nettie's had fallen, so, unashamed, the tears rolled down the cheeks of the woman who believed she had hardened herself to all emotion. She tried to speak, but could say nothing, and the doctor gently took her calloused little hand and held it in both of his.

After a while, she was able to say quiveringly:

"You know—you've already paid whatever debt there was. This ranch——"

"It's a homestead—a free gift of the Canadian Government. It'll not begin to pay for the cost of a man's education. A debt's a debt, and I trust you'll allow a man to wipe out a heavy obligation."

At that Angela smiled, though her eyes were wet.

"If you put it that way, Dr. McDermott, of course there's nothing else for me to do but to let you—let you—stake me—will you?"

"I will!" said the man, scowling at her as if very angry about something; and then he cleared his throat, and asked for a "bite of food for a hungry man who's been working day and night to hammer a bit of common sense into a bunch of farmers whose heads are made of wood."

Angela even laughed as she bustled about the kitchen, preparing a quick meal for the doctor, and when she set it before him, she asked:

"Who's sick now, doctor?"

"The whole country's nigh down," he muttered. "If they don't heed the warning I've been trying to hammer into their systems for months now, there'll be a sad lot of sick and dead people before the winter's out."

"As bad as all that?"

He replied solemnly:

"The situation could not be worse. Mark my words, if the plague comes up to the country from Calgary, where it has got a foothold already, our population will be cut in half."

CHAPTER XXVI

LIKE A THIEF IN THE NIGHT THE PLAGUE CREPT INTO ALBERTA. It came disguised at first in the shape of light colds, disregarded, but before the year was out, those neglected colds were to turn into that virulent scourge that singled out the strong, the fair and the young.

Calgary might have been likened at that time to a beleaguered city, on guard for a dreaded enemy attack. The widely printed warnings, in newspapers and on placards in public places and street cars; the newspaper accounts of the progress of the sickness in Europe, the United States and the eastern part of Canada, with the long list of death's grim toll, threw the healthy city of the foothills into a state of panic.

Schools were closed; people feared to go to church. Disinfectants were sprayed in all the stores and offices. Every cold, every sneeze was diagnosed as plague, and the mounting fear and hysteria awaited and perhaps precipitated the creeping enemy. For slowly, surely, pushing its way irresistibly over all the impediments and prayers to hold it back, the dreaded plague encroached upon Alberta.

The first definitely diagnosed cases came in early summer, which was raw and cold as always in that country. Only two or three cases were discovered at this time, but all of the medical and nursing profession volunteered or were conscripted for service to the city. Curiously enough, no means of protection were taken for the vast country that abounded on all sides of the city of the foothills.

The warm summer brought an abatement of the menace; but when the first chill swept in with the frosty fall, the plague burst overwhelmingly over the country.

Calgary, the city of sunlight and optimism, was now a place of pain and death. Scarcely a house escaped the dreaded visitor, and a curiosity of its effect upon its victims was that the young and strong were the chief sufferers. A haunting sense of disaster now brooded over the city. Hospitals, schools, churches, theatres and other public buildings were turned into houses of refuge. No one was permitted on the street without a mask—a piece of white gauze fastened across nose and mouth.

In this terrible crisis, the shortage of nurses and doctors was cruelly felt. An army of volunteer nurses were recruited by the city authorities, but these failed to supply adequate help for the stricken houses, and many there were who perished for lack of care and attention. The hospitals were crammed, as also were all the emergency places that had been transposed into temporary hospitals.

Despite almost superhuman efforts, the death lists grew from day to day. The ghastly sight of hearses, carts, automobiles and any and all types of vehicles, passing through the street freighted with Calgary's dead, was an everyday occurrence.

All of the surrounding towns had meanwhile also succumbed. In the smaller cities, the mortality was even greater, for here they had not the facilities and conveniences of the city, nor the skilled physicians and trained nurses.

Worst of all sufferers, however, were those who lived on farm or ranch, or at camps beyond the reach of help. Appalling was the condition upon the Indian Reserves, where the Indians died like flies. Ignorant and helpless at a time like this, forgotten in their misery by their white guardians, themselves cut down by the plague, they sought help at the farms and ranches, only to be turned away or bring the plague with them.

With half the country down with the sickness, Dr. McDermott applied vainly to the city and provincial authorities for help. He tried then to impress men and women from families not yet ill on the ranches into service, pleading that one should help the other at a time like this. That epidemic of fright which had so paralysed the panic-stricken cities, had now reached out to the farmers. Many in their desire to escape, shut themselves up in their homes, discharged their help and put up signs at their gates: "Keep away!" and they closed their doors in the faces of friends, only, later, to open them, in turn, to call for help. True, a few did respond to the doctor's call for help, but in nearly every case they themselves were overtaken, and the demand for help of any kind was so overwhelming that it was well-nigh impossible to do more than teach the sick to care for themselves.

Careworn, overworked, harassed and exhausted, worn out by lack of sleep and his work, Dr. McDermott stopped at Angela Loring's ranch.

They were coming in from the fields, the two girls, Angela in the democrat with the baby, and Nettie afoot, driving home a team of work-horses. They had been the one ploughing and the other repairing the broken fences. Despite the destruction of their crop, they were pluckily on the land again, preparing for the next year's seeding.

Dr. McDermott, bag on the step by him, watched them as they watered and fed and put up their horses for the night. Then, each taking a handle of the basket, they came through the barnyard to the house.

For the first time since she had known her doctor friend, he failed to greet Nettie with his cheery:

"And how's my lass to-day?"

Gaunt and haggard, he arose to scrutinize them gravely, before grunting:

"Hm! All right, eh? Not touched. Well, set down, girls. I've that to tell you that will make your hearts a wee bit heavy."

Dr. McDermott opened his black bag and took out some pills and a large bottle of disinfectant. These he set on the steps. Angela, the baby in her arms, her brows slightly drawn, looked down at the lined face of the doctor, and her own turned grave.

"Let's go in. You look as if a cup of tea won't come amiss. Let me pass. I'll make it at once."

"You'll hear me through first, and I've no time for tea. There's a bit of sickness running around the country. 'Tis the same they had in the old land. You'll put this disinfectant about your place, and on your person, and in case—in case of certain symptoms, you'll go straight to bed, and you'll stay there till I tell you when to get up, and you'll begin then to take at once the pills I'm leaving. What's more, you'll at once send Jake for me."

There was a pause, and Nettie's and Angela's eyes met.

"Needn't worry about me, doc," said Nettie. "I'm awfully healthy. You don't have to give me no pills."

"That's the ignorant sort of talk I've been listening to all summer; but the very ones who boast of their strength are the ones stricken."

"What are the symptoms?" interposed Angela.

"Symptoms! Fever, backache, headache, nose bleed and tendency to sneeze, hot and cold flushes."

Angela's face stiffened. Her glance went furtively from the baby to Nettie.

"Are there many down?" she questioned with assumed casualness.

"Thousands, ma'am, in the city, and God knows how many in the country."

"What are they doing for help?"

"In the country they are doing without it—shifting for themselves."

Angela looked startled, and Nettie turned slowly around, her gaze falling upon the doctor in silent question.

"Who's taking care of them, then?" she asked.

"They're takin' care of themselves. They creep out of bed and crawl to each other, and some of 'em die before they can get back to their own beds. In most of the families that have it, they are all down at once."

Angela said abruptly:

"Now look here, you've got to have some supper before you start off."

"No time for supper. There's nine in the Homan family down, including the help. I'm on my way now."

He had snapped his bag close. Nettie passed by him into the house. Angela paused at the door, clutched his sleeve and sought to restrain him from leaving.

"Now, look here, doctor, it won't do you a bit of good to try and take care of people if you don't take care of yourself first. You've got to eat. So you come right in. It won't take me a minute to fix something for you."

"No, can't stop. I had a bite at noon, and will reach Homan's in time for another sup."

"Well, wait. A minute or two more or less won't matter. I want to know about this. Can't you get nurses from Calgary, and aren't there any other doctors in the country?"

"There are three besides myself over my territory, but two of 'em's down, and the other!"—the doctor scowled and muttered something about "white-livered coward."

"And nurses?"

"I tell you I've been unable to get *anyone*. The city nurses have their hands full in town, and they won't come up to the country. As for the women themselves—the farm women—those who are not down—have gone plumb crazy with fright. I've gone from ranch to ranch like a beggar, imploring help."

Nettie had come out again. She had changed from her overalls to the blue house dress that Mrs. Langdon had made for her, and over this she had thrown the plaid shawl. She had her blue woollen tam that Angela had knitted for her on her head, and she looked very young and sweet. A few articles of clothing were knotted in a neat bundle under her arm.

"Doc," she said, "I'm going with you."

There was a long pause. Dr. McDermott blinked up at her, scowled, grunted something under his breath, and cleared his throat loudly. Angela stood stiff and still by the door, her arm closing automatically tighter about the baby.

"I'm awfully strong," went on Nettie, "and I ain't likely to catch nothing, and it don't matter if I do, far as that goes. You'll let me go, won't you, doc?"

"You're a good lass," muttered the doctor, "and you'll be a grand help to me."

At last Angela found her voice.

"Nettie, you're forgetting your—our—baby!" she said.

Nettie swung around with a curiously eloquent motion. Her bundle dropped to the ground and her hands twitched.

"No, no, Angel, I'm not forgetting him; but you'll be good to him, won't you? and he'll never miss me—even if I don't come back no more."

"Nettie Day, don't dare to talk like that," said Angela savagely. "I won't let you go if you have any thought like that in your head."

But Nettie did not hear her. For the first time since her baby's birth she was holding it in her arms, and the feel of the little warm moist face against her own brought a pang that was blent of both agony and joy. All of the mother in her seemed to at last surge into being, and her face was as white as death when she resigned it at last solemnly to Angela. The motion awakened the baby, and now its cry was more than she could bear. She clapped her hands over her ears and ran to the gate. Dr. McDermott picked up the bundle and followed.

CHAPTER XXVII

OF THE THIRTY OR FORTY MEN PREVIOUSLY EMPLOYED by the Bar Q, but two remained that winter—a Chinaman and Batt Leeson, at the Bull Camp. The foothill ranch was completely deserted. There was no one there but the Bull himself to care for the several thousand head of cattle.

When the plague reached the country regions, there was a general exodus from the ranches, for tales ran about the country of stricken men corralled like cattle in bunk-houses and barns, and left to shift and care for themselves.

That winter, the cattle in the foothills roamed the range like mavericks, rustling for their water and feed. They were, however, better off than the pure-bred stock at Barstairs; for the former were hardy stuff bred to the range, and the open fields had ample feed for them. On the other hand, the formerly pampered pure-bred cattle were used to care and nursing. They had been practically raised by hand and were accustomed to feed from the heaped-up troughs, where the attendants on hands and knees spread out their food. Now, penned in limited pastures and cattle sheds, where the ground was bare as stone, they were irregularly and spasmodically fed and seldom watered by the half-dazed and always drunken Batt Leeson.

Chum Lee, paralysed with fear of the "black plague," which had cut down all of his "boys" at the Bull Camp, lived in terror that it would overtake him also. Chum Lee had an aversion to death in the white man's land. He wanted to repose in peace upon the sacred soil of his ancestors. He would have run away from the camp, but the bare country with its vast blanket of snow showed no spot of refuge to which the Chinaman might retreat, and he feared Bull Langdon as he would an evil spirit.

Back and forth between the two ranches like a Juggernaut of fate tore the great car of Bull Langdon. That his men had died like flies; that three-quarters of the country was down with the plague, concerned not the cowman at all. What alarmed and incensed him was the fact that his cattle, the magnificent herd that he had built up from the three or four head rustled from the Indian cattle, roamed the range uncared for and neglected. Many of them, drifting before a bitter blizzard, had perished in coulie and canyon. Worse still than this was the deterioration of the pure-breds. The loss of a single head of this stock meant several thousand dollars.

Not alone his cattle obsessed Bull Langdon. He brooded unceasingly over Nettie Day. Almost it would seem as if she remained in his devouring mind to torture and to punish him for his crime against her, and the thought of the child she had borne him set him racing up and down like a caged beast. That child made her more than ever his, he gloated; yet how was he to gain possession of her? He knew that the "Loring woman's" words had not been idle, and behind the capture of this girl he craved, loomed the black walls of the penitentiary. In spite of that, he intended to have her. In spite of the world itself against him, he would have back Nettie Day. He would bide his time. Some day—the Loring woman would not always be on guard.

Nettie was nursing the stricken farmers. She, the pariah and despised of the foothills, was going from ranch to ranch caring for those who had condemned her. She had sat up all night soothing and ministering to aching heads and bodies. She had closed the eyes of their best beloved, and her tears had dropped upon the faces of their dead. In their hours of deepest anguish and agony, they had clung to her cool, strong hands, as to an anchorage of hope.

The country people had overwhelmingly reversed their opinion and judgment of Nettie Day. Indeed, they cared little what her past had been. She was their Nettie now.

By the end of January the plague reached its peak. Meanwhile, whole families had disappeared. Others were slowly creeping back into health and hope again. It would not be long, Dr. McDermott promised Nettie, before she would be free to return to her baby and her friend.

She began to count the days, and to scan the skies for that shadowy arch across the heavens that in Alberta precedes a "Chinook" and is the forerunner of soft weather, for Dr. McDermott was expected to come for her with the first Chinook. Nettie thought ceaselessly and yearningly of her baby. Away from him, he grew into visible being in her mind, and, heedless now of his paternity, she loved him with all the passion of her warm, young heart. When the Chinook broke up at last the fierce cold of that month, Dr. McDermott kept his word. Nettie, all of that day, trod on air. She was going home—to her baby!

When the doctor arrived, however, his face was grave. He carried a heavy heart with him. His labours were far from being over. The Bow Claire Lumber Camp had succumbed to the plague. Nearly a hundred men were down.

Calgary had promised help. Calgary had promised it before. Who, in all that wide-spreading country, would go deep into the heart of the timber lands to nurse the lumberjacks?

When the doctor's Ford chugged to the back door of the Munson farmhouse, where Nettie had been nursing, she was there to meet him, her old plaid cape about her and her woollen tam upon her head. Her face was aglow, and her eyes shone up at the doctor as bright as stars. He had telephoned her he would be around by noon, and she was to be ready and not keep him waiting.

Nettie had hugged and soothed the surviving three little Munsons; she had kissed the suddenly passionately sobbing and remorseful mother, and shaken hands with the husky-voiced father, who quite simply and reverently asked the Lord to bless the girl who had cared for them. To hide her own welling tears, she had run from those clamouring and crying children and shut the door between them. Now she was in the Ford, the robes tucked about her. Breathlessly she squeezed the arm of her old doctor friend.

"Oh, doc, just to think that I'm going home now—home to Angel and my baby! Oh, it's just heaven to be here beside you and on our way."

The "doc" had one of the new self-starters, and there was no need of cranking this year. They buzzed down the road in the "Tin Lizzie," making a great racket and leaving in their wake a cloud of smoke and odour of oil. For some time they went along in silence, and then Nettie came out of her happy mood of abstraction as she gradually noted the gravity of her friend's face. She touched his arm timidly, though her heart began to quake with misgiving.

"Can you really spare me now, doc?"

There was no answer, and Nettie pressed his arm, repeating her question.

"Can you, doc?" And then, as still he did not answer: "Is anyone else down now?"

"Nettie"—Dr. McDermott slowed up—he tried to make his face blank, for he did not intend to ask any further sacrifice of the girl beside him; nevertheless, he wished her to know the facts, "Nettie, the Bow Claire Camp is down."

"The Bow Claire!"

The colour had receded from her face. Her hand stole to her heart. "Cyril!" was her first thought; and then the doctor's solemn words sank in with their deep significance.

"Nearly a hundred men, Nettie, and not a soul to care for them."

There was a long pause. Dr. McDermott looked steadily ahead. The car was pounding and sending out jets of steam from the lately frozen radiator.

"Doc," cried the girl suddenly, breathlessly, "this ain't the road to Bow Claire. Turn your car around!"

"A promise is a promise," said the doctor. "I promised I'd bring you home to your child, lass, and I'll keep my word if you say so."

"But I don't say so. I don't want to go home—yet. I shouldn't be happy—even with my baby. My place is where I am needed most, and you should know where that is, doc."

"Dear lass," said the doctor gently, "they're needin' you sore at Bow Claire."

"Then turn your car around, doc, and don't you m-mind if I seem to be c-cryin'. It's just because I'm excited, and oh, I'm so g-glad of the chance—of—of the opportunity, doc, to go 'long of you to Bow Claire."

Dr. McDermott blinked through clouded glasses. Then he swung his wheel sharply around, backed along the slippery, thawing ground, and went over a culvert into a snow bank on the side of the road.

There was the grinding cough of the engine, and it stopped dead. Again and again Dr. McDermott started the car, and back and forth it chugged in a vain effort to pull out of the slippery snow pit. From under a pile of produce and baggage, the doctor produced a snow shovel, and began the process of "digging out," making a road before and behind where the ear might back and get a new start on to the road again. As he shovelled the snow, digging under and about the car, there was the honk of the horn of an approaching car, and over the grade suddenly came into sight the huge touring car of Bull Langdon. At the sound of the automobile horn, Dr. McDermott had straightened up, intending to ask for aid, but as he perceived whose car was approaching, with a scowl, the doctor doggedly resumed his digging.

In one comprehensive glance, Bull Langdon took in the situation, and the sight of Nettie cooled the fever that for days had possessed the man. She was visibly terrified by his appearance, shrinking back under the cover of the car, and that terror gave him a fierce delight and the old feeling of domination over her. He got down from his car and examined the place where the back wheel seemed wedged.

"Stuck, are you?" he gloated.

"We'll be out in a minute."

"Not on your life you won't. You'll not pull out of that to-day."

"Very well, if that's what you think, suppose you haul us out."

"Ain't got a rope, and my engine won't stand the gaff."

Dr. McDermott's wrathful stare met the unblinking one of the Bull. Then he turned his back upon him and applied himself with savage zeal to his task.

"Where you headed for?"

"None of your damned business."

"It ain't, heh?"

The Bull was in high humour now. His hand rested upon the Ford, close to where Nettie was shrinking back behind the curtain. His bold eyes held hers fascinated with a sort of terror. After a moment:

"Tell you what I'll do," he offered. "I'll take you aboard my car and pack you wherever you're goin'. You can 'phone the garage at Cochrane to send out and haul your Lizzie."

Dr. McDermott could not see Nettie, but he could feel the imploring words which in her fear of the Bull she dared not utter aloud. He knew that Nettie was crying out to him:

"No—no—never! I would rather stay here forever than go with the Bull."

He looked the cattleman up and down, with something of the cold stare and contempt that Angela Loring was able to achieve so remarkably.

"We'll pull out without your help," said Dr. McDermott curtly. "Don't need you. Don't want you."

"Hmph!" chuckled the Bull. He cut a chunk of chewing tobacco and bit into it. He spat, blinked his eyes at Nettie, and then buttoning up his big beaver fur coat, moved to his car. Climbing aboard, he grinned down at the girl, as he pushed his foot on the self-starter. There was the soft purr of the engine murmuring the quick response, and the great car slid along the way. As it raced along the road, something like madness tore through the being of the Bull. His pent-up desires of days and months found an outlet in this wild surge of emotions. The faster the car, the more the relief and sense of elation. He was telling himself that he would be back where the other ear was stalled when the night should have fallen.

As soon as the Bull's car had disappeared from sight, Nettie was out of the Ford.

"Oh, doc, he'll be back. I know he will."

"Let him. Nothing to be afraid of. Feel in the pocket of the car—no, the other one. Give me that——"

Nettie passed the revolver to him, and the doctor thrust it into his hip pocket.

"Now, lass, can you give me a hand?"

Together they pushed with might and main upon the car. It went up a few paces and slid back into the snow. Again they pushed, and at the doctor's order, Nettie found and thrust under the wheel a stone that held it in place. The Doctor then climbed aboard, and with Nettie pushing behind, it snorted forward a few feet, slipped back, jerked ahead again; there was a tremendous grinding, and the whirling wheel jumped over the side of the culvert. The car jumped forward. With a whoop of triumph, Dr. McDermott made room for Nettie, who climbed aboard the moving car. They were off again. Loudly clanking and making a terrific noise, the flivver flew along the crazy roads, panted up incredibly steep and slippery grades, plunged into snow fields and on into the timber land, where only the narrow cattle trails made a path through the woods to the lumber camp. They "made the grade" in two and a half hours of hard riding, and pulled into the dead camp with horn honking cheerily.

CHAPTER XXVIII

THAT MEETING WITH NETTIE ON THE ROAD more than ever fixed the Bull in his determination to again possess her. The exhilaration that had followed the meeting, and frustration of his hopes and plans, when upon his return he found that the little car had in fact pulled itself out and was gone, had turned to an almost crazed desire for the girl. It dominated all other feelings. His cattle, his ranches, his great money losses, the impossibility of obtaining help—even the palpable deterioration of his prized bulls at Barstairs—all these matters were now of no consequence, indeed literally shoved out of his thought by the one overpowering passion that consumed him.

Bull Langdon was incapable of love in a finer sense, but in his blind, passionate way, he was madly and tormentedly in love with Nettie Day. His passion for the girl was like a fire that burned and raged within, seeking an outlet where there was none. He was more a madman than a normal human at this time.

He thought of the girl ceaselessly, chortling with delight as he pictured her beauty, which had if anything developed. There was a new quality, however, in Nettie's beauty, a spirituality, a certain haunting light that was appealing and poignant; but Bull Langdon noted only that the summer's work in the fields had reddened her cheeks and brightened her eyes, and that her lips were like a scarlet flame.

If he pictured Nettie as she looked at him with her wide frightened eyes from the doctor's Ford on the road, his mind went back also to those other days when he had held the girl in his arms. Many a night as he tramped the floor of the empty ranch house, his half crazed mind went over and over again, a hundred times, those days when she had been under his power—like pure-bred stuff in the Squeezegate. She had been weak and docile then, a timid, terrified captive; but now there was a new expression in her face, a look that was like a shield—a warning guard that held the man back and warned him that if trapped again she would struggle to death. He told himself he did not wish to hurt Nettie—he wanted only to have her back where he believed she belonged by right. He would make her the second Mrs. Langdon, and at the thought—Nettie at the Bar Q—reigning in the great ranch house, keeping the place clean and sweet as his first wife had done—the Bull threw out his arms and clinched them back, as if in fact the struggling girl were actually within them, and he crooned words of savage tenderness, and then moaned and whimpered at the frustration of his desires.

His desperation made him resourceful and cunning. He sought Nettie Day at every farm and ranch in the foothills and the adjoining prairie country. No longer his car tore along the roads from Bar Q to Barstairs, intent upon the supervision of the demoralized herd. He was upon another hunt. The running to earth of a quarry whose price he set above all value.

Espionage of the Loring ranch revealed the fact that Nettie was not there, but lying in wait, in due time he captured and tortured the unfortunate Jake, son of an earlier passion than Nettie. He had picked up the breed on the trail, racing bareback upon some errand into the hills, and his questions as to the whereabouts of Nettie, after prodding and kicking, brought the information that she was "far way off on the hills. She at lumber camp. Everybody goin' die on Bow Claire."

That was enough for the Bull. He knew now where was Nettie Day, and the knowledge, instead of satisfying and calming him, had the opposite effect. Nettie and Cyril were there together. That was his sole thought. Murder crept into his soul. He had almost the outraged sense of one who had been cheated and wronged. Nettie was his! Why, she had even had a kid by him. That kid——

Nettie's baby brought a new force to his thought. An idea, electrical with possibilities, occurred to him. If he could not take this girl by force, there was one way by which she could be lured to Bar Q. He was amazed that he had not thought of this before. Human nature, he knew, was no different to cattle nature where young were concerned. The cattle mother would go through walls of fire to reach her offspring. What then would keep Nettie Day from coming to Bar Q, once she knew her baby was there? One needed not to throw the lariat upon the mother's neck. The roping of her child was all that was needed. Bull Langdon swung his car around.

CHAPTER XXIX

TWO "GREEN" HANDS WERE NOW AT BAR Q. They had been sent out by the Government Employment Office, and for several days, prior to his search for Nettie, Bull Langdon had been trying to break them in to the cattle "game." They were English, guileless, clean-cut youngsters, of good family, who looked upon the foully-swearing cowman as a pathological subject that both edified and amazed them. Their knowledge of ranching, or "raunching" as they called it, was of the vaguest, but they were good riders and the life appealed to their sporting sense.

One of the anomalies of the ranching country of Alberta is the wide difference in the type of people upon the farms and ranches. Where on one place may be a man who can neither read nor write, his neighbour, and often his chum and "pal," will be the son of an English lord, one of those odd derelicts that drift over from the old land, and adapt themselves to the ranch life, and more often than not return unwillingly to their homes. University men and agriculturists experimenting with irrigation projects and intensive cultivation; New York business men and men from other big cities in the States, who, for divers reasons, have broken away from the cities and gone in for farming on a big scale, raising the level of farming operations to that of a business, rather than a slovenly, weary process. For the most part, however, the farming population of Alberta is made up of that solid, plodding type that have trekked out from Eastern Canada or the mid-Western States, tempted by the cheapness of the land and the richness of the soil. These proved the backbone of the country. Between them are sandwiched colonies of peasants from the Scandinavian countries and from Europe.

A hired man on an Alberta ranch may be an illiterate clod of the old type; on the other hand, he may be a fresh-faced, college-bred son of a man of wealth and even title. Or again, some wayward wanderer, gone broke in the colony, and using up the remittance from home on drink and cards. There is also the type of English student and sportsman, who enjoy "roughing it," and who hire out both for experience and as a lark.

To this latter type, the men at Bar Q belonged. They had come up to Bar Q largely to escape the city of gloom and plague, and they were extremely anxious to remain at the ranch. The Bull, intent on getting away, endeavoured, in a few days, to teach them what he called the "A B C's" of ranching. They demonstrated their ability to remain in the saddle eight or ten hours at a stretch, and to ride over thirty or forty miles without undue fatigue.

The Bull showed them "the ropes"; pointed out where certain cattle were to be gathered in; indicated the fields where they were to be driven, and, promising to return in a few days, he rode off and left the "tenderfeet" in charge of the great ranch.

After his departure, the two young Englishmen rode over the place, marked the likely places for big game, took a "pot" or two at a yowling coyote on a hill; came over the pleasant hills and pasture land, back to the comfortable bunk-house, and decided that they had a "snap," and that "raunching" was the life for them. It was a jolly sight better than hanging around a small city up to its neck in sickness. In the warm spell that followed soon after the departure of Bull Langdon, the Englishmen "rode the range" like hunters, and their methods of rounding up cattle were weird and salutary in effect. They raced and chased the cattle, galloping along at top speed, thrilled by the spectacle of the fleeing herd which they persistently and doggedly sought to overtake. The experienced cow-puncher lopes along leisurely behind or alongside a bunch of cattle, taking care not to hurry his charges, for to run cattle is to "knock the beef off" them. That spring, the lean cattle of the Bar Q appalled the least sophisticated of ranch people, and it is certain that the guileless Englishmen never suspected for an instant that the blame belonged to them.

A cold spell following a thaw, the Englishmen gaped at the thermometer, which was dropping rapidly to thirty below zero, and retreated in a hurry to the warm bunk-house, fairly convinced that no living thing could survive such a temperature. A peculiarity of the Alberta climate is its rapid change from cold to warm and to cold again, but the Englishmen had thought that Chinook was the opening breath of spring. The unexpected bitter weather alarmed and appalled them. They spent the day shut up in the house, piling huge logs into the great square wood stove that spluttered and sent off an enormous heat. Also they concocted toothsome dishes—they were excellent fellows, as most Englishmen are, at "batching" and camping, and they knew how to cook. They had such game as venison, moose, mountain goat and sheep, to say nothing of the small game, mallard duck, prairie chicken, partridge, grouse, quail. These abounded in the wild woods of Bar Q, and the Englishmen had prudently "brought them down" while rounding up aforesaid cattle, the "killing" in fact contributing considerably to the flight of the terrified herd.

This game, expertly drawn to the ranch by horse sleds, was piled up frozen in the immense store room adjoining the bunk-house, where also was an ample supply of stores. It was certain that no matter how long the siege of Arctic cold might last, the hands of the Bar Q would survive starvation.

Shut in thus in the bunk-house, their days were by no means empty, for when not engaged in cooking or feeding the wood stove, they wrote articles on "ranching in the wild north-west," or indited epistles home to thrilled relatives, who had some vague notion that their dear ones were sojourning in Polar regions. Sometimes letters came from cultured and refined English people, whose knowledge of Canada was of the weirdest, warning the young men to be careful of the treacherous Esquimaux, and when they had time to run over and call upon a friend or distant cousin or uncle who was somewhere in their neighbourhood in Ontario or Nova Scotia. Their ignorance of the immense distances between the provinces of Canada was almost unbelievable. These dear folk at home, our young Englishmen took pleasure in thrilling with all kinds of stories, in which they shone as big game hunters and fishermen, to say nothing of how they moved, heroically followed by a band of noble red men.

CHAPTER XXX

WHILE ANGELA DID HER CHORES IN THE MORNING, Jake cared for the laughing, blonde child of Nettie. The breed adored the baby, and the happiest moments of his life were those spent in diverting the crowing and vastly pleased youngster. Angela had constructed a small yard, the four sides of which were made of smooth rails, about the height of the child, and in this space, nearly six feet square, the baby crawled and pulled himself about, sometimes rising to his sturdy little legs, there to crow triumphantly, ere he comically toppled over. On the outside of the yard, Jake, on hands and knees, played cat and dog.

Nettie's child was beautiful at this time, with his mother's fair skin and blue eyes, and blonde hair curled in tiny ringlets all over his small round head. He was the embodiment of good humour, and though he had never been strong, his health at this time was good.

Life had a new meaning for the woman recluse in these days. Something of the change was reflected in her expression. The defiant look was almost gone from the bright eyes, the lips were no longer bitterly compressed; with the slight colour in her cheeks, and her soft grey hair curling about her face, Angela Loring was almost beautiful, as she cuddled the baby in her arms and murmured foolish endearments to it.

By the time she finished her milking and chores in the early morning, the baby would be awake upon her return to the house, and, like all healthy youngsters, loudly demanding care and food. Before either Jake or Angela breakfasted, master baby must first be cared for. Full and satisfied, rosy and clean, he would be put in contentment in the yard, where he tumbled about among his favourite toys, clothespins and empty thread spools, which he rolled around the yard in high glee, or sucked or chewed upon with relish.

That morning in March, Angela's chores were long-drawn out, for, hard as she pumped, the water froze before dropping, and the barn was full of stock, which had come up from the frozen pastures to the shelter of the sheds. There were twenty or thirty head hungrily hovering in the shed, and seeking their share of the food and water, reserved generally for the special milking stock and weak stuff interned in the barn. She worked hard and valiantly, driving back the greedy steers and rescuing a half-frozen calf, which barely escaped death under the scampering heels of the larger animals.

Examining the foundling, she decided it would be necessary, in order to save its life, to bring it to a warmer place than the barn. She made, therefore, a rough sled of a couple of boards, and by pulling and pushing, managed to shove it under the motionless animal. Attaching a lariat to the boards, she pulled the sled with the calf upon it over the frozen ground to the house.

Jake did not respond to her calls to open the door, and she was obliged to push it open herself, letting in an icy blast. She tugged and pulled at the sled till it slid into the kitchen, and the calf was deposited by the roaring fire. Breathing heavily from the exertion and holding her sides, she leaned against the table, and as she leaned, suddenly she saw Jake. He was lying face downward on the floor. Her first thought was that he was suffering from the convulsions that periodically attacked him, but a moment later her startled glance fell upon the empty yard. Her senses whirled. It seemed as though everything began to swim around her, as slowly her knees gave way and, for the first time in her life, Angela Loring fainted. But it was only for a moment. She came back to consciousness all too soon, and crawled on her knees to where Jake, now moaning and moving his head, still lay stretched upon the floor. His horribly bruised face was contorted and grey, and when he opened his eyes the blood ran out of them. She knew then that Jake had been struck down and beaten.

"Him! Him!" gibbered the breed.

"Jake, what has happened? Where's the baby? Oh-h!"

"Bebby—all—a-gone. Him—the Bull take a baby! Him gone away."

Again the world began to spin about her, but she fought against the faintness. Feeling her way to the door, Angela Loring went out into the bitter cold again, to the barn, where the mare with her new colt whinnied as she slipped the stock saddle across her back. She trapped the colt in an adjoining stall, and then as she got on the mare's back, she whispered to the animal:

"Go swiftly, Daisy, or you'll not get back to your baby."

There was a long snorting whinny from Daisy, an outcry of protest at leaving her colt, and an answering equally indignant cry from the little creature in the stall.

The nearest telephone was five miles from Angela's ranch, and when she rode into the farmyard, in spite of the intense cold, the mare was sweating from her wild race across the country. The astonished farmer who showed Angela the 'phone—for it was the first time she had been known to step into any house other than her own—stayed by the door and listened with pricked-up ears as the excited woman called Dr. McDermott at Springbank. By a merciful coincidence he answered to that call, and a few minutes later, the farmer at the door was obliged to help his strange visitor to a seat and to call in a hurry to his wife for help.

For again Angela Loring had fainted. Her first question when she opened her eyes and looked up at her neighbours' faces, was:

"Has he come? Has Dr. McDermott come?" and when they replied that he had not, she wrung her hands and broke into weak tears.

CHAPTER XXXI

THE UNEXPECTED RETURN OF THE "GOVERNOR," as sardonically the Englishmen had named Bull Langdon, was an exciting event in a life hitherto quite pleasant. He arrived late on a March afternoon, the snort of his engine and the honk of his horn arousing the hands from a siesta, where, stretched before a raging wood fire, they drowsily smoked and read.

They took their time putting on warm fur coats and overshoes before answering that continued summons, and, sauntering out presently, smiled good-humouredly at the shouting cowman.

"Here you! Take this in. Ain't no fire to the house. Want it thawed out."

The first of the Englishmen, whose long name need not appear here—"Bo," is what Bull Langdon called him—took the bundle in his hands, and then almost dropped it, for something moved within it, and a sound that was like a suffocated moan arose from that package of mystery.

"My word! The thing's alive, d'you know!" exclaimed the startled Englishman "Hang it all, man, I believe it's a baby"!

"Take it to the bunk-house," roared the Bull, backing into the garage. "Thaw it out."

Gingerly carried by the amused "Bo" to the bunk-house, and deposited upon the cot that he himself had but recently reposed upon, the low moaning cries continued. Both the little bare feet had kicked out from the sheepskin coat, and were frozen stiff. One little fist stuck out of the coat, and there was a great swelling on the forehead, where he had struck when he had rolled from the seat of the car to the floor. Nettie's baby was otherwise bruised from the cruel bumping of the long, mad ride from Yankee Valley, a distance of thirty-five miles.

"Cutey," the name sneeringly imposed upon the other Englishman by Bull Langdon, because of his scrupulous dress and an extraordinary monocle, now stuck that despised piece of glass in his right eye, and amazedly surveyed the crying child. Though, in truth, the cries were getting fainter, and a sort of frozen rigour was creeping over the child.

"Well, what're you gapin' at?"

Bull Langdon was glowering in the doorway.

"Where in the world did you pick the little beggar up?" inquired "Bo."

"It ain't none of your business," was the surly retort. "He's here, and he's here to stay. He's mine, and he's got my brand upon him."

"You don't mean to say that you brand babies in this country! Never heard of such a thing! It's damned inhuman, I should say."

"Don't matter what you say or think. I want that kid thawed out. Give'im something to eat. He's cold and hungry, but he's healthy young stuff and 'll pull through. Kids ain't no different to cattle. Feed 'em and keep 'em warm. That's all they need. He's bawling now for food. You got something handy?"

"Nothing but a bite of cold venison. Hardly the stuff for a baby."

"He ain't no baby. He's a yearling. Here!"

He had torn a strip of the venison from the piece, and had thrust it into the hand of the child. The tiny fingers closed feebly about the meat, and then dropped limply away. The eyes, so like his mother's, opened brightly, wide and blank, and then the white lids shut out the light from them forever.

"Gone to sleep," grunted the cowman. "Keep the fire goin'. Thaw him out and feed 'im. That's the stuff. He'll come round. He's good stuff. I'm off for the timber. Be back soon. You ain't much good neither of you at tending to cattle. So I'll give you a nursemaid's job. Let the cattle

Cattle

rustle for themselves. You concentrate on—" He indicated with a jerk of his thumb the now utterly still child of Nettie Day.

Alone, the two Englishmen continued to look at each other speechlessly. Presently said the one the Bull named "Bo:"

"Well, I'm hanged—utterly hanged! What's to do?"

"Carn't say any more than you can. Blamed if I know the first thing about a baby!"

"Cutey" was looking down sentimentally at the small blond head now.

"He's awfully quiet, isn't he? Doesn't seem"—he touched the tiny head. It was cold as ice, and all of a sudden the two men looking down at the little frozen form realized that the baby would never cry again.

"By Jove!" whispered the one. "The little beggar's dead, I think."

Their eyes met meaningly.

"What's to do?"

"Gad, I wish I knew."

"It's a dashed serious matter."

"Rather!"

"I'll plug over to the house and telephone. Where did he say he was going?—er—to Timber something. Now I wonder what his telephone number might be?"

"Try 'Information.' She should know."

"Information" knew of no Timber number, but when the stuttering Englishman made clear to her that there was a dead baby at Bar Q, she connected him swiftly with the Provincial Police Station at Cochrane, and a voice at that end, after a series of irritated questions, suddenly briskly said that "they'd look into it," and Bo hung up.

The charmed "raunching" was gone for the Englishmen. All the rest of that afternoon they sat in sombre silence in the bunk-house, carefully averting their glance from the small, covered head. Their appetites gone, they could not prepare the usual evening meal, and contented themselves by drinking strong tea that boiled at the back of the stove, and smoking steadily.

It was nearly dark when the sound of a motor along the road was heard, and the laboured panting of the car as it climbed the steep grade to the ranch. The men, relieved, looked for the police officers, but, in fact, the solitary mounty who had been dispatched upon the case was coming by horse twenty-eight miles from the ranch, and would not arrive for several hours. When the Englishmen opened the door of the bunk-house, they were surprised to see a woman running swiftly ahead of the fur-coated doctor, whose acquaintance they had already made.

Their first thought was that Angela was the mother of the child, and this thought, indeed, they still had when she threw herself down by Nettie's dead baby and burst into unchecked and heart-rending weeping.

CHAPTER XXXII

CHUM LEE PACKED EVERYTHING HE POSSESSED in the world in the capacious bamboo bag, slipping in between the articles of clothing, bottles and pipes and boxes filled with redolent odours. He muttered and chattered frantically to himself as he packed, and his hands shook like those of one afflicted with ague. Finally, he tied and knotted the stout rope about the bag. Trembling and shivering, he put on the old sheepskin coat, muskrat cap and fur mittens. His bag upon his back, Chum Lee scuttled hurriedly from the Bull Camp at Barstairs.

That bitter morning, he awakened from a long doze, in which he dreamed of summer seas, green as jade, of colourful sampans, alive with moving, friendly faces; of a girl's face, oval and soft, with gentle almond eyes and a smile like a caress. Her hair was black and smooth as the wing of a teal, and there were bride's flowers on her head. That fair vision of his home and his young wife he had left in China vanished into the cruel mists of memory. He awoke to intense cold, the blackness of death itself which reigned in the one-room bunkhouse. With a sob, the Chinaman crept out of bed, scurried across the room, ascertained that the fire was out, and staggered to the wood box. On his way back to the stove, his arms loaded, he stumbled across something that lay on the floor in his path. A loud cry escaped the Chinaman. The wood dropped from his shivering arms and clattered down upon the Bar Q "hand." Batt Leeson lay upon his back, where he had rolled out of his bunk overnight. His mouth and eyes were wide open, but they were intensely still, for Batt was in his last long sleep.

The sight of the dead man, the last of his "boys" to succumb to the "black plague," was too much for the overwrought and drug-filled Chinaman. Even the terrors of the zero weather were less appalling to face than what was within that shack. Between chattering teeth, Chum Lee sent up frantic appeals to the gods of his ancestors to lift the dead curse which had befallen the land in which he had sojourned too long.

As he went out of the gate, the long wild roars of the hungry bulls followed him, and, turning back upon a sudden resolution, Chum Lee shoved the bars along the sliding doors. He would perform a last act of charity and win the favour of the gods. The famished brutes within would come up presently against the loosened door. They would be free from the prison wherein they had been penned for days.

That day the long hungering bulls, bellowing and moaning their unceasing demands for the withheld food and water, crushed up against the doors, and, as the Chinaman had foreseen, the gates gave way. They stepped across a barrier of logs. Heads lifted, they sniffed along the corrals, found the bars down where the Chinaman had lifted them, and strayed forth to the lower pasture. Here the gate yawned widely opened to the highway. On all sides the wide-spreading country, deep in its mantle of heavy snow, told a tale of unspeakable desolation. Out into the world, in search of that which had been denied them in the luxurious cattle sheds that had cost Bull Langdon several thousand dollars to erect, went the famous Hereford bulls.

Pampered and petted, used to softening care, knowing no range save the sweet home pastures. how should they fare in the wilderness? Now the cold of the implacable winter smote them to the bone, and that unbroken expanse of frozen snow, four feet deep, rose in mounts and hillocks on all sides of them.

Nibblings there were none. The streams and the rivers were frozen hard. The wretched cattle, huddling together, swept along the road, before a blinding wind that came from out the hill country, the prelude of a coming Chinook, but with the first blast intensifying the cold and sapping the last bit of strength from the famished and lost cattle.

They drifted blindly before the wind, driven against fence lines and trapped in coulie and gulch. Great white flakes began to blow like fairy birds, drifting in a dazzling sunlight. They fell like a million feathers over the huddled herd, and buried them under a mighty mound.

He who was once known as Prince Perfection Bar Q the IV., of whom the great specialist had predicted he would startle the pure-bred world, was the only one of all that noble herd to survive. Facing the west wind like a gladiator, the Prince turned from his fellows, and defiantly trod his way through the storm to where the shadow of the hill country loomed with its promise of shelter and feed. Sniffing along the road allowances, pausing only to bellow his immense moans, the massive brute pursued his way.

CHAPTER XXXIII

THERE WAS A CELEBRATION AT BOW CLAIRE. Lanterns hung from rafter and eave to give the place an air of festivity. Across the back of the big lumber camp, where the fifty-five men who had pulled through were now convalescent, bright Indian blankets and bunting were hung.

Now, when the last of the men had been pronounced out of danger, with the connivance of the doctor and an Indian, the lumber-jacks had smuggled into the camp the requisites for the intended celebration.

When Nettie came from the foreman's house that evening to make her nightly rounds of that emergency camp hospital, the surprise party awaiting her almost frightened the girl. A dozen accordeons were going at once; mouth organs were slung from one side of the mouth to the other; Jim Crow, the only darky in the camp, grinning from ear to ear, had a real banjo twanging, and Mutt, a giant Russ, with a voice like a tremendous bell, led all hands in a deafening cheer for Nettie, a cheer that, in spite of their weakness, they kept up for a long time.

Nettie faced her "boys," startled and moved beyond words, and though the tears ran down her cheeks, she smiled through them. But the ceremonies were by no means over with the cheering and singing. Thin, pale, his eyes shadowed by a haunting look that fairly scalded the girl's heart, Cyril Stanley stepped forward, a bouquet of flowers in his hands.

He alone in all that camp had been unable to find the courage to speak to Nettie. Those flowers, ragged from their journey on horseback, had cost the Bow Claire Camp more than the flowers of a prima donna, and they were meant to speak a message to the girl that services more beautiful than a song had evoked. Cyril had begged for the privilege of being the one to present the flowers. He came slowly forward. Looking Nettie steadily in the face, the first time that he had dared steadily to look at her, Cyril extended the flowers; but the words he had planned to speak died on his lips. He could not even whisper her name.

She took the flowers from his hands, and her pure gaze sank deeply into his own. For a long moment, while the camp looked on in entranced silence, those two estranged lovers looked into each other's faces, and in that moment, all of the fog and doubts cleared from Cyril Stanley's mind. Something within him seemed to burst, breaking down all the dikes of hatred that he had so bitterly erected. He knew, as he looked into Nettie Day's clear eyes, that he loved her still beyond anything on earth, and that he could have sworn by the God above them, that she could do no wrong; that her heart was clean and pure and undefiled.

Upon the hush that had fallen so strangely in that lumber camp, suddenly a new sound broke—the clear, crisp, metallic ring of a horse's hoofs without. Slowly the girl with the flowers in her arms turned as pale as death.

His chin thrust out, his big knotted hands swinging like a prize fighter's, half drunk with alcohol and furious desire, Bull Langdon burst into the camp. His glance swept the circle of still weak men, then turned to pinion the unhappy girl, from whose arms the flowers had dropped to the floor. Even before he spoke, a comprehension of the truth flashed like a miracle over Cyril Stanley. Never would Nettie Day need now to speak one word of explanation to her lover. Over Cyril there rolled a flood of memories, shaking his being with a realization of the damnable crime that had been wrought against the girl he loved, and which death alone could now wipe out.

"So here y'are," said the cattleman. "You come along with me, gell. Your baby—and *mine*, gell, is at Bar Q. He's needin' you more than this bunch of bo's."

Suppressed sound was strangled in the throat of Cyril. He leaped fairly into the face of Bull Langdon. Staggered by this unexpected onslaught, and then perceiving who it was that attacked him, his lips drawn back like those of a gorilla, Bull Langdon fell upon Cyril. Down went the boy. He tried vainly to rise, but, weak from his long, recent illness, he could barely reach his knees before the cattleman sent him spinning to the floor once more.

There was a low, murmuring rumble about the camp, the hoarse, cursing protest of the lumberjacks. It grew into volume and intensity as the Bull laid his hand on Nettie Day, and burst like a tidal wave when she broke through his grasp and fled through the open door.

He found himself surrounded by a mob of madmen. Cursing and weeping because of their weakness and inability to pull down the man they raved to kill, they leaped and struck at him. Back to wall, he struck out right and left with his mighty fists, sending one man after another staggering to the floor, and meanwhile craftily edging nearer and nearer to the door through which Nettie Day had fled.

CHAPTER XXXIV

IT WAS A STILL, COLD NIGHT. Through the pathless dead timber lands fled Nettie Day. She was on horse, for on leaving the camp she had the presence of mind to mount the Bull's own mare, left standing without the camp. On and on she urged the great animal, heeding not the cut of the snow-laden brush and boughs that snapped back against and whipped her face and head.

A vast silence reigned in those dense woods. Not a twig stirred on the frost-freighted trees. No living foot seemed to move within the depths of the forest. All that she heard—if she heard aught at all—as she fled like the wind through the timber land, was the sound of her horse's hoofs crunching upon the frozen snow. On and on, indifferent to the penetrating cold, intent but upon one purpose, to reach Bar Q before the Bull should overtake her, and there gain possession of her baby.

The mare was built on big, slim lines. Of thoroughbred racing stock by her sire, she was the foal of a Percheron mare. She was, therefore, swift as well as strong, and she bore the girl throughout the night without a pause all of the twenty miles to the Bar Q.

The dawn was breaking over a still sleeping land, and a great shadowy arch spread like a rainbow across the city, the long-prayed for symbol of Chinook weather. Before the day should be half gone, a wind would blow like a bugle call from the mountains, and, racing with the sun, would send its warm breath and mellow beams upon the land. But Nettie Day saw not that omen of sunny days. Cramped and cold from her long ride, with a speechless terror tearing at her heartstrings, she fell rather than alighted from her horse, staggering toward the house, at the door of which Angela Loring stood, with empty arms.

Meanwhile, another kind of drama had taken place in the timber land. Bloody and battered from his fight with the lumberjacks and loggers, Bull Langdon sought the trail. In these deep woods, so still and silent, with the spell of the night upon them, in spite of the deep silence, there was the feel of live, wild things hidden in bush and coulie, couching and peering through the snow-laden brush.

He knew the country well, and had somewhat the sense of smell and instinct of the cattle themselves. He had boasted that he could "sniff his way" anywhere through the foothill country, and that his long years of night riding had given him cat's eyes. Although the woods were dark in the clearings the moon shone bright as day.

It was twelve miles to Morley, an Indian trading post on the edge of the Stoney Indian Reserve. By turning from the main trail and following an old cattle path, he could cut the distance by a third.

The white moon wavered behind moving clouds, anon lighting the paths and darkening them. The cattle trail went in a wavering line toward a valley that ran along the Ghost River, where was the summer range of the foothill cattle.

If the woods were still and dark, the valley, flooded with moonlight, seemed like a great pool, a theatre on the far edge of which dark forms wavered and moved. These were the stray cattle that had escaped the fall round-up. Now they found shelter from the inclement weather in the seclusion of the deep valley, sheltered by the hills on one side, and with the rapidly flowing Ghost upon the other.

The first impulse of a cattleman, when spotting stray cattle on the range, is to ride close enough to them to read the brand upon their ribs; no easy matter in the night; but the Bull was used to brand-reading at night. He was halfway across the valley, when a certain restless stirring apprised him of the fact that he was seen. Range cattle will move blindly before a man on horse. It is a reckless man who will risk going near range cattle afoot. The bawl of a leader of the herd sent the cowman cautiously back to the shelter of the brush. He was unprepared to risk a stampede, but he marked the place where the cattle strayed and made a mental note to round up in a few days.

He was now but four miles from Morley, still travelling along the edges of the woods, when suddenly a low, moaning call, growing ever in volume and power, till it swelled to a mighty roar that shook the bristling branches of the trees, smote across the still night, reverberating and echoing back and forth from the hills on all sides.

Stock still the cattleman stood, his head uplifted, his ears pricked up, straining. Well he knew that great, far-reaching bellow, which aforetime had swelled his breast with pride— the outraged challenge of the champion bull. Somewhere, close at hand, hidden in those dense woods, Prince Perfection Bar Q the IV. was at large.

There was no more sound or sign from the brute, and when at last Bull Langdon came from out the sheltering woods, there lay before him a wide field that flanked on one side the Banff Highway, on the other side of which were the fenced lands of the Indian Reserve.

As he had moved through the thick woods, pausing ever and anon to listen to the sound of a tread behind, of a breath of that low, menacing murmur that preceded the alarming roar, the cattleman's overwrought fancy pictured the bull upon his trail. It was not merely a premonition, but a fearful certainty that close upon his tracks that live, wild thing was following.

The open field was before him. A swift dash across it to the road, and across the road to the line of Indian fencing, where lay assured safety from his terrible pursuer. An instant he hesitated, and then, head down, like one of his own cattle blindly driven, went the cowman.

Not swiftly enough, however, for the Hereford bull who had trailed him.

On the edge of the timber land, Prince Perfection Bar Q the IV. stood in lordly question, his stern eyes fixed upon the moving speck before him. Slowly he marked his prey. Then, head dropped, he came on with a lumbering yet lightning gait, directly, unerringly toward the goal he sought. Back turned to the charging bull, madly intent upon reaching the shelter of the barbed wire fences on the south side of the highway, the cowman saw not what was behind him.

The great bull shot across the field like a released bomb from a colossal catapult, sideways, on the run, his dropped head swinging. His horns smote the hapless cowman directly in the ribs. There was a horrible rending. Into the air Bull Langdon rose, to fall to earth like a stone, there to be lifted and tossed and gored again and again till all that was left of Bull Langdon bore no more resemblance to a human being than a mass of pulp.

Here was a terrible justice in which the hand of a master avenger might almost have been perceived. Yet the Hereford bull had gored but the man's body, while Bull Langdon had gored a woman's soul.

CHAPTER XXXV

"LASS," SAID DR. MCDERMOTT, his hands resting upon the shoulders of Angela Loring, "in the old land I was but a puir lad, and you the grand young lady of the manor house. But here, in Alberta, we're nought but mon and woman, and as such, I'm asking you to be my wife."

She answered by simply drawing down his hands and placing her own within them.

"It's a puir rough sort of a mon you'll be getting," said the doctor huskily. She shook her head, smiling at him through misty eyes.

"Angus," said Angela softly, "I'll be getting the salt of the earth!"

Hat twisting in his hands, outside the barn Cyril waited for Nettie. As she came out, a pail of milk in either hand, he gently took them from her and set them upon the ground. He had learned that speech by heart—the speech he was going to say to Nettie; but now, as they looked into each other's eyes, no words were needed. As instinctively as life itself, they moved to each other. Nothing on earth now mattered save that they were in each other's arms.

In the house, hand in hand, they faced their friends, and, immersed in their own joy, noted not that the doctor's arm was about Angela's shoulders.

"Nettie and I are going to get married in the summer," said Cyril simply.

"Why wait for the summer?" rumbled the doctor. "Angel and I are going to Calgary to-night. Come with us."

"'Twill take a month or two to rebuild the home again," said Cyril wistfully.

"Why build again?" said Angel softly. "There's *this* house for you, Cyril. It's our wedding gift to you and Nettie. I'll be going———" she smiled and blushed like a girl, but finished the words bravely—"to my husband's house," she said.

THE END

ACKNOWLEDGEMENTS

The Invisible Publishing team would like to thank Dr. Mary Chapman and the team at The Winnifred Eaton Archive for their encouragement and guidance. Our hope is that this new edition will help foster the aims of The Winnifred Eaton Archive to keep the work of this fascinating writer available for a diverse set of readers. We encourage all interested readers to visit the archive at **winnifredeatonarchive.org**. We would also like to express gratitude to the family of Winnifred Eaton Reeve for their support.

This new trade edition of *Cattle* coincides with the centennial of its first publication in Canada and we have used the Canadian edition as our source text. The publication of this edition also coincides with a centennial conference—Onoto Watanna's *Cattle* at 100: Indomitable Women in the West During Chinese Exclusion—held in Calgary in July 2023. We would like to thank Dr. Lily Cho, a conference keynote speaker, for introducing this new edition.

THE THROWBACK SERIES reintroduces public-domain books to contemporary readers, continuing the vital work of keeping Canadian stories alive and available. Our Throwback books also give back: a percentage of each book's sales will be donated to a designated Canadian cultural or charitable organization.